'A witch and a diplomat. That's a dangerous combination.'

Gaby felt a tremor of nervousness. She quelled it. 'I don't see how I could possibly represent any danger to you.'

'Don't you?' he murmured.

'No, I don't. It's ridiculous. But if you don't want me here, you have only to tell me to go.'

Her eyes met his. His expression was quite unreadable. At last he said softly, 'Yes, I can do that.'

'Well, are you going to?'

'Not just at the moment.'

Dear Reader

Hej — Hello and welcome once again to Euromance! This month we are inviting you to Sweden, the perfect setting for a love story, with its abundance of fresh air and scenic wide open spaces. Sophie Weston takes us to a beautiful rural area of the country where the pace of life is seductively leisurely and relaxed. . .so be prepared for a romantic journey that is bound to take you away from it all. . .*Adjö*!

The Editor

The author says:

'As a schoolgirl I had a Swedish penfriend who taught me that Swedish children quite expected to speak other languages fluently and to travel and work abroad when they grew up. It was my first introduction to a true internationalist!

'I have learned that Sweden is a land of great contrast: the harsh beauty of the northern landscape compared with the baroque frivolities of Stockholm, the lively folk-art tradition with the austere and haunting contemporary arts.'

Sophie Weston

★ TURN TO THE BACK PAGES OF THIS BOOK FOR *WELCOME TO EUROPE*. . .OUR FASCINATING FACT-FILE ★

ICE AT HEART

BY
SOPHIE WESTON

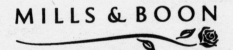

MILLS & BOON

MILLS & BOON LIMITED
ETON HOUSE, 18–24 PARADISE ROAD
RICHMOND, SURREY, TW9 1SR

*First published in Great Britain 1994
by Mills & Boon Limited*

© Sophie Weston 1994

*Australian copyright 1994
Philippine copyright 1994
This edition 1994*

ISBN 0 263 78505 X

*Set in 10 on 10½ pt Linotron Times
01-9406-55375*

*Typeset in Great Britain by Centracet, Cambridge
Made and printed in Great Britain*

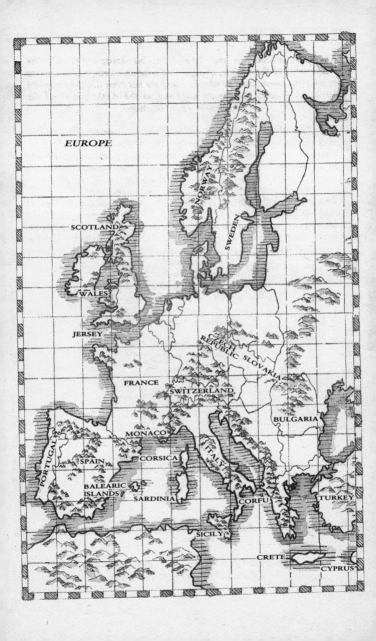

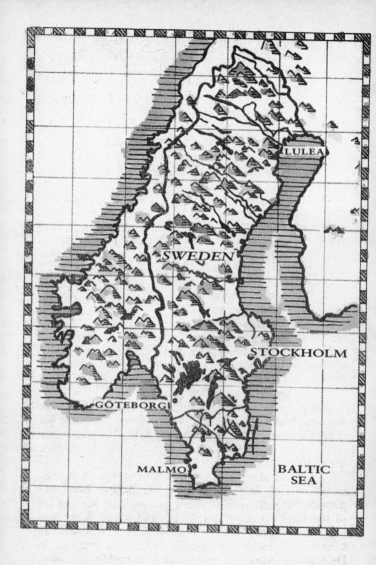

CHAPTER ONE

'I'M SORRY, Miss Hyssop. Your father won't keep you a moment,' said the polite personal assistant.

Gaby Hyssop chuckled. She had never visited her father when he had not kept her waiting. His assistants were usually instructed to ply her with magazines in which he was admiringly interviewed. They would also bring her coffee, the quality of which was designed to make his only daughter regret her decision to live in London when she left music college, rather than join her father in Los Angeles as he had asked her to do.

'Something to read?' the girl offered.

Gaby bit back a grin. Its cover displayed a photograph of Michael Hyssop, alternative practitioner to the stars, with his arm round an adoring beauty. The fact that the woman was on her third come-back and was a self-proclaimed ex-alcoholic only made it the more interesting from Michael's point of view, Gaby thought. Presumably he'd had a hand in her recovery.

'Thank you,' she said gravely.

The girl gave her a relieved smile and went back to her computer screen. Gaby pulled the long rope of her shining chestnut hair over her shoulder and sank down on to a sumptuous couch to read about her father's triumphs.

There was nothing particularly gripping in it, she found as she flicked through the pages. Both her parents were alternative therapists and she knew a lot of the theory from her mother. But while Anne was interested in deep healing and experiment, Michael ran a more successful and highly publicised practice in Hollywood. Anne, an intense and unworldly creature, was frankly scathing about it.

Gaby was rueful, remembering. Her mother had run out of patience with Michael and his love-affair with the media some years ago. In the last furious row, which Gaby still could not remember without wincing, Anne had called him a shallow showman. That was just before she walked out, leaving him in LA and bringing their only child home to London.

Gaby considered his photograph now, her head on one side. He was still a fine-looking man, she thought.

The telephone on the girl's desk buzzed. She answered it. By the way her voice instantly warmed, Gaby knew who it was on the other end of the telephone. Could you dazzle someone over the telephone? she mused, as the girl put down the instrument with a far-away look in her eyes and turned to her.

'Mr Hyssop says would you like some real American coffee?' she said.

Gaby laughed aloud.

'Doesn't change, does he?' she said with affection. 'No, thank you. I'll carry on reading his Press notices.'

The girl gave her an uneasy smile and went back to her work. Gaby selected another magazine. Michael or someone had marked one of the glossy gossip column snippets in a red biro. She ran her eye over it without much interest.

Dr Sven Hedberg, the distinguished brain surgeon, is now consulting the uptown practice of Michael Hyssop, aromatherapist to the stars. Dr Hedberg, who is an international authority on electrical activity in brain cells, suffered a tragic accident in his native Sweden last year. Ever since he has been troubled by occasional numbness in his right hand which has cut his operating schedule.

Popular Michael Hyssop won acclaim from the medical fraternity last year when his unorthodox treatment restored the use of martial-arts star Sergei Josten's left arm. Doctors had given him up after an accident on set left the twenty-six year-old star with seemingly permanent tremors. Sergei is currently shooting *Champion from Hell* for Blane.

Handsome Sven Hedberg, who is lecturing in California for a semester, must be hoping Michael can do the same for him.

Hedberg, thirty-nine, was an Olympic cross-country skier when he was at medical school. Maybe that was when he developed his taste for international beauties. A noted heart-throb in his native Sweden, he has most recently been seen around town escorting gorgeous Oriana Meadows. Wedding-bells are not imminent, though. The dashing bachelor is known to value his freedom.

Gaby raised her eyebrows. It was more usually her mother who worked with doctors. Michael's chosen clientele was more glamorous. Though Dr Sven Hedberg certainly sounded more glamorous than podgy little Dr Bailey, she thought with a sudden grin. Dr Bailey worked at King's and quite often referred patients to Anne. He was dedicated and imaginative but she could not imagine him cross-country skiing — or dating film stars. Maybe Dr Hedberg was not so out of character for Michael after all.

The phone rang again. The girl answered it, listened for a few moments, then, with a small murmured apology to Gaby, left the room. She looked, Gaby thought, worried.

Gaby put down the magazine and stretched. She should really be practising, she thought. She flexed her hands, running them over an invisible keyboard. She was not practising enough. But the need to pay the bills was keeping her waitressing most of the day. Three evenings a week she played the piano in a West End restaurant. She gave piano lessons too but the summer holiday season was coming up and too many of her

pupils left London. That meant she would have to do
more waitressing; or playing in nightclubs. Which
meant less practising.

She got up, restlessly. It was very frustrating. It was
not even as if her career was not taking off; she was
doing better than she had ever dared to hope when
she'd launched her career as a soloist. It was just that it
was not very well paid. . .*yet*, she told herself. Gaby
was by nature an optimist.

She began to wander round the room. It was much
as she had expected — large displays of hothouse
flowers, a soulful portrait of Michael and one of his
more famous film-star clients in a silver frame on an
occasional table, invitations and messages strewn everywhere. This was the paraphernalia of the travelling
celebrity alternative healer. A leather-bound appointments diary sat on the Louis Quinze-style table his
assistant was using.

Gaby glanced down at it idly. Someone had scored out
the afternoon in pencil with her name written across it.
Someone else, however, had inserted two appointments.
One was with a television company. Screwing her head
round so that she could read the entry, Gaby deduced
that these were the people who were still with Michael.

He would have to hurry, she thought, amused. He
would have to get rid of them soon if he was going to
keep his next appointment with Dr S. Hedberg at four-
thirty. And when he was going to fit his daughter in was
anybody's guess.

The door from the corridor opened. Gaby turned
round without much interest, assuming that she was
being plied with coffee after all.

But the man who came in was no pleasant waiter
with a tray. He was tall and powerfully built, she saw
as the door swung to behind him. He was dressed in a
dark suit that moulded his body in creaseless, expensive
perfection. As he turned to her she saw a thin face with

elegant bones, a mouth of sculptural perfection and deeply lidded eyes. He was startlingly handsome.

He was looking preoccupied, frowning slightly. Otherwise his face was expressionless. Watching him, Gaby could not have said why she had the immediate conviction that he was in a towering rage, but so strong was the impression that she took a step backwards involuntarily.

His eyes lifted at the movement. They were as grey as stormy sea; and as cold. They surveyed her. They swept her up and down so that she put a nervous hand to her rope of hair to check whether the plait was unravelling, as it so often did. His eyes took note of the nervous movement. There was no change in their expression, except perhaps the coldness intensified.

He doesn't like me, thought Gaby, startled out of her own preoccupations. There was no reason why he should, of course. But she was not used to encountering such immediate disdain in a stranger's eyes.

'Michael Hyssop,' he said curtly. 'I have an appointment. The desk sent me up.'

So this was the next name in the book. Gaby squinted down at it again. Dr S. Hedberg. Why did the name sound familiar? And what was there about him that made him so formidable?

Gaby reminded herself that it was foolish to be intimidated by a man you had only just met. So she smiled pleasantly and said, 'I'm afraid he's engaged just at the moment but. . .'

Dr S. Hedberg clearly did not think much of that. He was impatient and not taking the trouble to disguise it.

'He sought this interview, not I. I have no time to waste. You can tell him I will wait exactly five minutes.'

His eyes were a peculiarly icy grey. They seemed to cut through her like a north wind. Where *had* she heard the name before?

He said, 'You're not his usual girl, are you? Does he have one in every port?'

Gaby flushed. 'What's that to do with you?' she said on a flare of unusual temper.

'If you were Hyssop's usual assistant you would know that I mean what I say. I'm not waiting around while he holds court. I have a paper to deliver to the Western Hemisphere Neurosurgery Conference tomorrow which needs my attention. If Hyssop isn't here in five minutes it will get it sooner than expected.'

Of course. *That* Dr Hedberg. Gaby's indignation was temporarily submerged in curiosity. Cross-country skiing, freedom-loving bachelor Dr Sven Hedberg! Well, now she had met him she could see why he was a bachelor. No woman would put up with that air of icy command long enough to marry him.

He was surveying her with cold exasperation. 'Do you understand?'

Gaby nodded. She was briefly nonplussed. 'But ——'

'Just tell him,' he advised gently.

She said uncomfortably, 'I can't do that. You see ——'

She met his eyes and experienced something of a shock. They were implacable. He looked as if he were going to war, Gaby thought suddenly. As if he were facing his enemy. It shook her.

'I suggest you do, however.' It wasn't quite a threat but it made Gaby stand up very straight all of a sudden.

She said coldly, 'I understand you were due at four-thirty.' She looked pointedly at the grandfather clock in the corner. 'In which case you are early.'

He didn't spare the clock so much as a glance. 'Changed his mind, has he?' he said grimly.

'I don't know what you mean.'

His eyes narrowed. 'Or did he have a different plan?'

Gaby stared, uncomprehending. But in a moment his meaning became all too clear. The cold eyes swept over her. He pursed his lips. It was a slow, explicit assessment that sent the blood storming into her cheeks.

'Impressive. Big brown eyes, perfect skin and hair

for a prince to climb up into your tower,' he said softly. It did not sound as if it was intended to be a compliment, but its effect was extraordinary. All of a sudden she became aware of her height, of the sensitivity of her skin, of the supple strength of her slim body, of her long-fingered hands resting on the open diary. Gaby swallowed. No one had ever made her so conscious of her body, she thought in confusion. Not even Tim, all those years ago, had made her feel so utterly invaded as this man did just by looking at her. Her very skin tingled as if he had physically touched her. She had never experienced anything like it in all her twenty-four years.

She glared, hating him. He stared back, impassive. She could see why the gossip columns had bothered with him. He had the body of an athlete and the harsh, handsome face of an eighteenth-century rake.

Then suddenly, like sunlight after a dark storm, he looked genuinely amused. It transformed him.

Not handsome, Gaby thought in confusion. Devastating.

'And a temper.'

He strolled over to her. To her own private fury, Gaby gave ground. Bewildered, she found herself retreating before him as if she too had unexpectedly come upon an enemy. Some part of her brain was watching her behaviour with critical self-contempt; but her immediate reaction was of the imperative need to be wary of this man.

'No, no, not like that, darling,' he said mockingly. 'If you glare at me like that I shall think you want me to go away.'

He put out a hand and touched her face lightly. She shied away.

'No,' Gaby said chokingly.

'No, I thought not,' he said.

She knew he was misunderstanding her deliberately. It seemed part of this inexplicable battle between them.

She swallowed. But before she could speak he had taken her rope of hair in one hand and slid the other round her thin shoulders.

'If you've been told to be nice to me,' he said, his breath warm against her horrified lips, 'the way it's done is this.'

And his mouth touched hers.

Gaby choked and tried to push him away. The hand between her shoulderblades became insistent. She felt as if his body was a mountain wall and she was being crushed to death against it. All the old wariness rose up. With it, mercifully, came an anger like fire.

'Let me go,' she spat as she tore her mouth away.

He gave a soft laugh. His amusement was total, thought Gaby in outrage. She freed a hand to strike that handsome, laughing face. But he caught it before she had more than half formed the thought.

He forced it down. Taking both her wrists in a light clasp behind her back, he held her immobile against his body. With his free hand he tipped her pointed chin and forced her to look up at him. Gaby met his eyes reluctantly, her own smouldering.

'I do not encourage ladies to hit me,' he said smoothly. 'It gives them a mistaken sense of possession.'

'What?' Gaby was as bemused as she was angry.

He touched his lips to her own in an insultingly brief contact. Something deep in her breast contracted in a slow, sweet shiver. It shocked her, almost as much as the man's unwarranted behaviour. She tried again to haul herself away from him.

He did not let her go. Instead he held her for a moment, breast to breast, looking down thoughtfully into her angry eyes. A gleam came into his own. He bent his head.

'Not a risk in your case, I admit.' He was murmuring it against her bewildered mouth. His voice was husky. Just the slightest hint of an accent had suddenly become apparent. 'But the point is always worth making,' he purred between little kisses that made Gaby shut her eyes against the whirling world. They did not seem to be having any effect on him at all. 'Women can build so much out of so little. Don't you agree? Mmm?'

And then he was taking possession of her in an uncompromising kiss that set the whole world rocking off its axis.

The shivering in her breast became a full-scale earthquake. The powerful embrace was all too familiar. She was remembering too vividly. She was also remembering exactly why she did not like being kissed and how she had avoided it over the last three years. Gaby's eyes snapped open. She began to use her full strength against him.

It was at this juncture that, over his shoulder, Gaby saw the double doors to Michael's sitting-room open. Her father came out. He was looking worried. But as soon as he saw them he stopped dead. All expression was wiped off his face at a stroke.

She made a small, suffocated sound.

Very slowly the stranger raised his head. Gaby found she was shaking. It was a small satisfaction to see, as he released her plait, that there was a faint tremor in her opponent's hand as well.

Michael watched, his face a mask. Dr Sven Hedberg nodded to him unconcernedly. He did not seem to think it strange that he was still holding a flushed and indignant Gaby in his arms or that it needed explanation. He smiled down at her kindly.

'There,' he said. She could see he was laughing although his expression stayed solemn. 'If you want to keep the opposition sweet, that's how it's done.' The accent had completely disappeared.

Gaby was scarlet. She could feel the heat under her skin. She pressed the back of her hand to her cheek, hating him.

But she managed to say, 'Thank you,' in arctic tones.

'You're welcome,' he said, amused. 'And now. . .'

'And now Mr Hyssop appears to be free,' she snapped.

She saw Michael's eyebrows rise. Sven Hedberg stepped away from her. Not as if he was ashamed of being found kissing a strange girl in a hotel ante-room, Gaby thought in dudgeon, but as if she had suddenly become irrelevant. He seemed almost to have forgotten her.

All the amusement disappeared from his face. 'So he is,' he said quietly.

Michael's face tightened. Silently he half turned, indicating the room behind him. The stranger strode across to it and went in without a backward look. Michael followed him.

In disbelief, Gaby watched the doors close on her, leaving her alone in the waiting-room again. She sat down shakily. She could feel her blush subsiding, but the feelings didn't disappear so quickly. Not the indignation at the stranger's insolence; not the annoyance at her own behaviour. Not the bewilderment or the cold, tremulous excitement that his touch had somehow ignited.

It was unfamiliar and more than a little unnerving. Gaby had formed the habit of keeping men at a physical distance. She had her reasons for it and it was not a policy she often regretted. Now, however, she found herself wishing passionately that she had more experience to draw on. It would have been nice to play Dr Sven Hedberg at his own game, she thought wistfully, to fight ice with ice. Instead of that she had melted into a little warm puddle of sensation at his feet.

'I must be out of my mind,' Gaby muttered, ashamed of herself.

Didn't she have every reason in the world to be afraid of a man who touched and took without consulting anything but his own inclinations? *Excitement*? It was crazy. She had to be crazy.

She became aware of noises beyond the elegant doors. It did not sound like a civilised professional discussion. It sounded remarkably like her father's voice raised in anger. It surprised Gaby. Michael never lost his temper.

She went over to the door and knocked. There was no abatement in the angry voice. She hesitated briefly. The voice rose. Shrugging, she stopped knocking politely and went in.

A surprising sight met her eyes. Michael was sociable and sophisticated. His patients adored him only marginally less than his glamorous assistants did. Gaby had never before seen her father backed into a corner, looking harassed.

'Out of the question,' he was saying in the loud, hectoring tone Gaby remembered from the marital disagreements before her parents had parted. 'There was absolutely no guarantee. . .'

'Mr Hyssop,' said the stranger in a soft voice that was somehow more menacing than Michael's shouting, 'I am not talking about your so-called cure. I didn't have much faith in it, as you know. I have been to world specialists, after all.'

So the treatment that worked for martial-arts stars had not worked with the famous doctor, Gaby deduced. She found she was not altogether surprised, though she could not have said why.

'When it didn't work I wasn't surprised,' he went on, echoing her thoughts. 'I don't complain of it. I knew what was involved and I chose to make a fool of myself on the one per cent chance that it might make a difference. I am entirely responsible for that. It is not the point at issue. I am talking about the invasion of my privacy.'

Michael looked even more worried.

'I can explain. . .'

'Not,' said Sven Hedberg, 'to my satisfaction.'

Her father drew himself to his full height. His

opponent looked down at him in contempt. Gaby
winced at the expression. Silently she went to her
father's side and put a hand on his arm. Michael
covered it with his own almost blindly.

Michael said placatingly, 'Look, Hedberg, be reasonable. I'm sorry about the mix-up. But if you're honest,
you'll admit you have no reason to complain. I did
everything I said I would.'

'And so much more,' marvelled Dr Sven Hedberg in
a voice that froze Gaby to the marrow. 'How flattering
to find myself in the Hollywood magazines as well. You
didn't think to tell me about your Press release, I
suppose? It just slipped your mind?'

He really was very tall, she thought with a slight
shock. Her father was not a short man and the stranger
towered head and shoulders over him. The harsh, bony
face had deep lines carved beside the aquiline nose, as
if by pain or tragedy. The fox-red hair was marked with
wings of grey at the temples but if anything that made
the strong face look younger.

Young and fit and spoiling for a fight, Gaby thought,
biting her lip. Her fingers tightened on her father's arm
in silent support.

Michael said quietly, 'There was no Press release.'

'Then where did that article come from?'

Michael looked unhappy.

'It was no coincidence,' the other man pursued
ruthlessly. 'You asked me whether I would be interviewed on alternative therapies. I said quite clearly that
I would not. That was the end of the matter. Or it
should have been.'

'Dr Hedberg. . .'

'But it was too good an opportunity for publicity for
you to miss, wasn't it? Doctor with international reputation failed by medical science. I'm surprised you
didn't write the headline for them.'

Michael stood quietly under the ice storm of invec-
tive. But at that he shook his head.

'Of course I didn't give it to the papers. I'm sorry it got out and I admit that to some extent it was my fault but. . .'

'It was a breach of professional privilege,' Hedberg said coldly.

There was a silence. Gaby held her breath. Michael was looking sick.

'Don't you think you're over-reacting a bit, Hedberg? I mean, taking it to the courts. . .'

Sven Hedberg gave a harsh bark of laughter.

'You don't have any idea of professional ethics at all, do you, Hyssop? You call yourself an alternative practitioner. You're no sort of practitioner. You don't have the first idea about your duty to your patient. Well, it's time someone taught you. And if nobody else has, I will.'

Michael looked stricken. 'It was a mistake,' he said despairingly.

Gaby's heart turned over at the note in his voice. He didn't deserve the mauling this man was giving him, she thought, indignant. Hedberg did not even allow him space to defend himself. She couldn't bear it.

'Michael,' she said.

They were both startled. Michael looked down and his hand tightened painfully on her own. He was holding on to it as if it were a lifeline, Gaby thought in compassion.

Dr Hedberg looked at her through narrowed eyes. He took in the clasped hands. An expression of extreme cynicism entered the handsome face.

'The little helper, right on cue,' he said drily. 'You're sharper than you look, darling.'

Gaby stiffened. 'I beg your pardon?'

'If you can't divert the opposition, break up the fight. Well done. Do you get a lot of practice?' The insult was blatant.

This was her chance to say some of the things she had thought of only after that outrageous embrace. She gave him a glittering smile. 'Not a lot, no. At least, I've never been accosted by a perfect stranger before.'

Michael looked down at her in astonishment. He had never heard that tone from Gaby. Anne was the fiery one in the family, Gaby the peacemaker.

He said swiftly, 'This is Dr Sven Hedberg, darling. You must have heard of him.'

Gaby considered him. 'I don't think so,' she said with pleasure.

It was the truth, at least until she had read that article. It was also profoundly enjoyable to be able to puncture the ego of this arrogant monster.

Dr Sven Hedberg's eyebrows lifted slightly. He did not seem particularly cast down by the fact that she had not heard of him, Gaby thought.

'You relieve my mind,' he said coolly. His eyes met the gleaming challenge of hers and he gave an odd little bow. He spoke over her head to her father. 'I trust this is not another international beauty I shall find myself having escorted?' he drawled. 'Miss — er —— ?'

Michael was still looking down at Gaby. His expression was complicated. He held her eyes compellingly.

'Gabrielle Fouquet,' he supplied at last.

Gaby jumped. What was Michael doing, using her professional name? Clearly he was suspicious of this man.

She looked back at Sven Hedberg, hating him. 'Not unless you ask first,' she told him with a smile like a knife.

His eyebrows rose even higher. His eyes travelled up and down her slender form in an inspection as leisurely as it was insulting. A gleam that she had reason to know came into the wintry grey.

Excitement, Gaby thought. It made her shift where she stood in a flicker of inexplicable alarm. It was as if he had brushed the clothes away from her body; and touched her.

'If you can persuade Mr Hyssop not to take it to the papers, I might just do that,' he told her softly. The languid invitation was no compliment.

Gaby's temper went up like a bush fire. 'I wouldn't go out with you to save my life,' she told him fiercely; and with no great originality.

Michael said hurriedly, 'Yes. Well, we can continue our conversation another time, Hedberg. Now that Gabrielle is here, if you see what I mean.'

The tall man looked her up and down. Gaby felt a blush rising. Then he shrugged. 'I do indeed.'

'Perhaps we could get together tomorrow?' suggested Michael.

'There is no point,' Hedberg said flatly, 'It is in the hands of my lawyers. There is nothing more to be said. I have no intention of changing my mind.'

His eyes swept over Gaby again. She felt as if she had walked into an iceberg.

'No matter what the inducements,' he added. 'Good day.'

And with an abrupt nod he was gone.

In the resulting silence Gaby expelled a long breath. 'Phew,' she said, staring after him. 'What was *that*? An ice storm?'

Michael dropped her hand and went to a small table where he poured himself a generous measure of Scotch. 'Probably the worst mistake of my life,' he said, unwontedly grim. He swallowed a large gulp of the drink. 'I'm sorry you walked into that, chicken. He's an angry man.'

Gaby could not forget the ice blast that had stripped the clothes off her and been lazily appreciative of what they had found.

'He's horrible,' she said with a shudder.

Michael looked surprised. 'Do you think so? Most of the girls seem to fall over themselves about him.'

'Which girls?' said Gaby scornfully.

Michael looked faintly embarrassed. 'The girls at the centre.'

'Groupies waiting to group,' Gaby said dismissively. 'They're falling over themselves about some guy's sex appeal most of the time. Usually yours. It's what you pay them for.'

Michael's receptionists tended to be young and star-struck, hugely impressed by his famous patients. It was one of the things Anne was particularly scathing about.

Her father looked at her, swallowed the rest of his drink and poured himself another. 'Sometimes you can sound very hard,' he complained. 'At your age you should be doing a bit of falling yourself.'

Gaby repressed a shudder. 'Not my scene,' she said firmly.

Michael was clearly glad to be distracted. He shook his head. 'It's not right. A young girl like you. What are you now? Twenty-five?'

'Twenty-four and still on my feet,' she said. 'Emotionally speaking. And don't change the subject. What on earth have you done to cross Erik the Red?'

Her father looked amused. 'You are talking about a world authority on brainwave patterns,' he corrected. 'Genius of the age. Nobel prize contender. Not a Viking raider. Except where women are concerned, I suppose,' he added thoughtfully.

Gaby repressed the desire to seek further information on Sven Hedberg's depredations among her sex.

'And what did you do to get him mad?'

'Treat him.' Michael was wry. 'He was in some sort of accident in Sweden. That's where he comes from. Apparently there was a disaster at sea and he was in the water for six hours. When they fished him out his hands couldn't stop shaking.'

Gaby thought suddenly of the tremor she had detected when she was in his arms. So much for him being swept away by uncontrollable passion, she told

herself ironically. Then she realised the implications of
that faint involuntary movement.

'And he's a surgeon?'

Michael met her eyes. 'Quite. Oh, it's not permanent. It only happens when he's tired. And eventually
it should stop altogether. Nobody knows when, though.
Because nobody knows what's causing it. And in the
meantime he's had to cut his operating schedule drasti-
cally.' He gave a sudden laugh. 'The Swedish specialists
say it will clear up by itself in time. But Sven Hedberg
isn't a man who waits for things to happen by
themselves.'

'But why on earth did he come to you?' said Gaby,
frowning. 'I mean, there must be people in Sweden.'

'He was at UCLA for a term and Bob told him about
what I'd done for Sergei Josten.' He shrugged. 'I think
he looked on it as a bet on an outsider. No harm done
if it didn't work. But unfortunately. . .'

'Someone told the papers,' Gaby supplied. She loved
her father but she had few illusions about him,
especially when it came to publicity. 'Was it you?'

'Do I look suicidal?' countered her father indignantly. He sighed. 'No, it was Marcia. She thought it
would be good for the practice. She's not terribly
bright. Of course I explained about patients' rights to
privacy when she first came but I'm not sure it sunk in.
My patients don't normally want privacy,' he added
fairly. 'The more column inches the better for most of
them.'

Gaby nodded. It was fair.

'Have you sacked her?'

Her father looked uncomfortable. 'I know I ought
to. But she thought she was helping. And I can see how
she made the mistake.'

'If you sacked her you could tell Hedberg you'd done
so and that would shut him up.'

'Her husband walked out on her and she's bringing
up two small children without support,' Michael said

evenly. 'It's not her fault she's not bright. I'm not going to sack her unless I'm told to by a court.' He added with irritation, 'I don't know why the man is being so damned unreasonable. The article didn't say anything that was damaging. And it was all true. But he's got some hang-up about the Press, apparently. So he's just going to be bloody-minded unless I can think of a way of heading him off.'

Gaby nodded sympathetically. 'I take it the therapy didn't work?'

Michael frowned. 'Well, that's an interesting point. In the beginning it seemed as if it did, a bit. We gave him acupuncture. And aromatherapy and harmonics. He seemed to be responding—very gradually, of course. But then——' he flung up his hands '—it seemed as if he started to block it. Of course, that's easy to say. Hedberg pointed that out. And maybe it was only wishful thinking that it was working in the first place. But. . .' He sounded dissatisfied. 'Anyway, he said he didn't want to go on with it.'

Gaby was intrigued. However much salesmanship Michael might put into his pitch to the media, or even some of his patients, he didn't usually lie to himself.

'Frustrating for you.'

'Mmm. If it had worked, even Hedberg wouldn't be out for my blood.' Michael shrugged. 'Oh, well, nothing I can do about it at the moment. Let's forget it. Tell me what my beautiful daughter has been doing instead.'

Gaby smiled. 'Well, I'm not setting the Thames on fire,' she said. 'I've had three concerts with the quartet and we've been asked to do a European tour next season. I've been working with Christofsen on his new concerto.' She grinned suddenly. 'And I'm waiting in the Green Earth at lunchtime and doing my "Sexy Siren plays piano at In Camera" when Carlo books me.'

Michael looked concerned. 'I wish you'd let me make you an allowance. I can afford it easily.'

Gaby shook her head. They had been through this

before. 'If I'm not good enough to earn my living as a professional pianist, then I'll have to do something else. But thank you.'

'It doesn't sound like much of a living at the moment,' he said shrewdly.

Gaby made a face. 'Well, the teaching dries up in the summer. I'll be back on track in September.'

He laughed. 'Done any more music therapy with Anne?' he asked casually.

She shook her head. 'Not for a while.'

'Are you any good?'

Gaby laughed. 'Ask Mother. She keeps asking me back. Of course that could be just because she doesn't know any other pianists as cheap.'

'Hmm,' said Michael thoughtfully. 'And when are you next playing at this café?'

'Restaurant,' Gaby corrected him. 'In Camera, it's called. Very discreet. Very expensive. Tonight, actually.'

'I'll come along,' said Michael, making a decision. 'It's time I heard you play again. And I can take more Cole Porter than that modern stuff you like so much. It sounds like iron filings to me.'

'Philistine,' said Gaby cheerfully. But she gave him the restaurant's business card before she bade him a fond farewell.

She was nevertheless a little surprised to see him that night. He often had sudden inspirations of which he thought better later. He came in around eleven with the after-theatre crowd.

Michael was looking ten years younger than his age in his dinner-jacket and crisp frilled shirt, Gaby thought. She waved to him over the piano. It was clear that the adoring brunette with him thought the same. Unsurprised, Gaby recognised the personal assistant she had met earlier.

What did surprise her — and surprised her so much

that she almost stumbled in her playing — was that Sven Hedberg was also one of the party.

There was a note waiting for her at the eleven-thirty break. Would she join Mr Hyssop's table? Gaby sucked her teeth and decided that if Michael could endure the man so could she.

But her greeting was not friendly when Michael said, 'And Sven, of course, you've met.'

She nodded. Like the other men he had stood up at her approach. He towered head and shoulders over them all, she saw. He smiled at her with open mockery.

'Hyssop tells me you are multi-talented, Miss Fouquet,' he said smoothly.

Gaby looked at him with dislike.

'Michael's hardly an independent judge,' she said curtly.

Sven's eyes went from her to her father and back. The expressive eyebrows went up.

Michael said hurriedly, 'I liked that little jazz treatment of Barbara Allen. Did you write it?'

'The word is improvise, darling,' Gaby said. 'It comes out different every night. Just like me.' And she twirled the long Indian scarves that she used to dress up her plain black T-shirt and leggings.

She knew she sounded brittle and affected and did not care. Under Sven Hedberg's sardonic gaze she had the urge to behave just about as badly as she could. She kissed Michael on the cheek.

'I'll have to renew the war-paint before I play any more. See you.'

She looked round the table, carefully skimming her eyes over Sven Hedberg's amused countenance, and included them all in an airy wave.

'I'll call you,' Michael said after her as she danced away.

When he did, the following morning, it was with a shocking suggestion.

'I need your help, Gaby,' he said without preamble.

'I've got to get Hedberg to calm down. I'm sure he won't bring charges when he's had time to think about it. Last night he agreed to take some additional therapy.' He paused. 'He was asking whether you worked with me. I said yes.'

'I'm no therapist,' Gaby said with quick foreboding.

'You've worked with your mother,' Michael objected. 'She's as good as you get.' He stopped, then went on seriously, 'Look, chicken, I think what's wrong with him is he's too self-aware. He's a man who's used to being in control. So he keeps trying to monitor his own recovery. And that stops it. If we can get him doing something that he has to concentrate on, it might just break that barrier.'

'And it might not.'

'Oh, sure. But it's worth trying.'

'For whom?' asked Gaby drily.

'For Hedberg. And me. Come on, Gaby. You know you're always short of money through the summer.'

Gaby sighed. 'I may be. That doesn't mean I want a mad Viking storming up to my practice-room every day.'

'Maybe he won't be mad with you,' Michael said blithely. 'He seemed quite taken, I thought. I never caught him kissing any of the receptionists.' He sounded amused. 'Go on. Where's your spirit of adventure?'

'I save it for teaching piano to five-year-olds,' she said drily.

Michael changed tack. 'Look, this is serious, Gaby. I'll fight that case if I have to. It was an honest mistake after all. But it's going to cost a fortune. And frankly, I don't think Marcia can take it. What would it cost you to take the job on? You could even try and give the man a more generous perspective. It would only be a few weeks. You could stop waitressing.'

And do some of the much overdue practice, thought Gaby, torn.

In some ways it sounded ideal. If only the man had
not kissed her. Or if only the kiss had not filled her
with that treacherous, unfamiliar excitement.

'You can always cancel the sessions if they get too
much for you,' Michael urged.

Gaby sighed. 'All right,' she said reluctantly. 'As
long as he knows I'm a musician, not a therapist. And
as long as you supervise the whole thing.'

'Done,' said Michael. 'You won't regret this.'

'I wish I were as sure of that as you are,' Gaby
muttered.

But he had already put down the phone. She shivered
superstitiously. Her instincts were telling her she was
making a mistake. A serious mistake.

Her instincts proved to be all too trustworthy. Next
day she got an unexpected phone call.

'Miss Fouquet?' said a strong, clipped voice she
recognised, then, before she could answer, 'I have been
talking to Hyssop,' Sven Hedberg told her crisply. 'I
understand you are available to conduct a course of his
so-called music therapy.'

'Music therapy is very good,' began Gaby hotly,
having been impressed by her mother's results. Too
late she realised it sounded as if she was endorsing it
unreservedly and Michael as well.

'I hope so, for your sake and for Michael Hyssop's,'
he said. He did not even try to make it sound unlike a
threat, Gaby thought indignantly. 'I have agreed to
make a trial of it for a month.'

Well, she thought in relief, at least that put a period
to her time in purgatory with this alarming man. If he
came twice a week for a month, that made a maximum
of twelve hours that she had to spend with him. She
could manage twelve hours without either hitting him
or running away from him, she assured herself.

'Fine,' she said with equal curtness.

'I shall be going back to Sweden immediately, so we
will not be able to travel together,' the gravel voice

continued without emotion. 'If you give me your address, I will have my secretary mail you your tickets.'

Going back to Sweden? Travel?

'I don't think I understand,' said Gaby faintly.

'You will have to come to Sweden. I explained that was essential.' He sounded impatient.

Gaby found her temper beginning to rise. 'Not to me.'

'Of course not.' He sounded faintly astonished; presumably at the thought of negotiating anything with her, Gaby concluded.

Was that because he saw her as her father's puppet or because he didn't expect a woman to have a sensible approach? She decided that it was the latter. It did nothing for her temper.

'I had not expected to come to Sweden,' she told him with a crispness to rival his own.

'Does that mean you refuse?' The man sounded barely interested.

Gaby would have given anything she possessed to say yes and bang the phone down. But Michael needed her help. There was no real choice and she knew it.

'It means I will make my own arrangements,' she said. It was a token protest. 'Tell me when and where I should arrive.'

'My secretary will be in touch.' Gaby thought he sounded amused all of a sudden.

She knew that amusement. It grated across her nerves. She set her teeth and reminded herself it was only a month.

'It is some way from Stockholm. You will need to be met. I will give her instructions.'

Just as you've given me mine, thought Gaby in high indignation.

'Thank you,' she said coldly.

There was no doubt. He was certainly laughing at the other end of the phone.

'My pleasure. I look forward to seeing you in Sweden, Miss Fouquet.'

CHAPTER TWO

BEFORE the threatened secretary could get in touch, Gaby rang her father.

'What do you mean, Sweden?' she exploded as soon as he came on the line. 'How are you going to keep an eye on his treatment? I assume you're not coming too?'

Michael made soothing noises. It did not disguise the fact that she was right. He was not coming too.

'I can't give him music therapy on my own,' said Gaby, truly alarmed.

'You're committed now,' Michael said. 'I've got his cheque.' He told her a fee which made her blink. 'I'll send a messenger round with a therapy programme. Ask your mother if you're worried,' he added, inspired.

He rang off while Gaby was still trying to find words to express her feelings.

She rang back but he had gone into a meeting.

'Fine,' Gaby said grimly to the placatory personal assistant. 'Tell him he's paying for my air fare. First class,' she added, thinking of the exorbitant fee.

The girl laughed. 'I'll tell him,' she promised.

So when Sven Hedberg's secretary rang she was able to tell her that she was making her own travel arrangements.

'Dr Hedberg is expecting you on Monday,' the woman said, sounding worried. 'You are going to his house in Dalarna. It is a beautiful area, where all the lakes are, but it is a long way from Stockholm. You will have to be met.'

'Wonderful,' said Gaby drily. A long way from the flight back home if things went wrong, she thought. 'I'll let you know the time of the flight.'

It was a tight squeeze but she managed to be ticketed

30

and packed in time for the early morning flight on Monday. She was also supplied with both parents' suggestions on the course the therapy should take.

Anne had been intrigued.

'Doctors are terrible patients,' she had said. 'The therapist has to sneak up on them, so to speak. They get very bad-tempered because they're not in control. You will have to woo him when he's not looking, Gaby.'

Gaby had shuddered at the thought. Her mother had laughed. 'You'll be all right, darling,' Anne had said with what Gaby thought was totally misplaced confidence. 'You're very intuitive. You'll know what to do.'

'And if I don't?'

'The Lord will provide,' Anne had said with serene assurance.

'I don't find that very comforting,' Gaby had replied grimly. 'Give me an idiot's guide.'

Anne had looked displeased. But she had written down a suggested programme in her large loopy writing. It gave Gaby more comfort than all Michael's neatly typed pages.

Nevertheless it was an apprehensive Gaby who sat in the cool first-class lounge, awash with free newspapers, free orange juice and miles of thin-striped navy blue carpet. As far as the eye could see the room was full of men in dark suits with briefcases, or glamorous women power-dressed and made-up to professional standards. Gaby, with her long chestnut hair flying free from its recent washing, and jeans and trainers, could not have looked more out of place.

But when she was presented with a questionnaire, seeking her opinion on Scandinavian Airlines' customer service, she firmly put down her purpose of journey as business. A grey suit, looking suspiciously over her shoulder, sniffed.

Gaby gave him a rakish grin. For a moment he looked taken aback. Then he too smiled. She thought he might be going to speak but then their flight was called and she found she was nowhere close to him on the plane.

She saw him again, however, at Stockholm Airport. They came out from Customs side by side and he smiled at her again, this time with more intent. She was not entirely sure she liked the intent or the cold assessment she saw in rather reptilian eyes. But he was polite enough.

'Have you been to Stockholm before? Do you need any help?' he asked as she looked round.

Gaby shook her head, the long hair swinging. He looked at it admiringly. She drew back a little.

'I don't think so. I should be being met.'

'Of course,' he said, as if he would not have expected anything else. 'People who wait for passengers are usually through here.' And he lifted her canvas backpack from where she had dropped it casually at her feet and put it on to his own trolley of matching luggage.

'Oh, don't,' Gaby protested. The man made her oddly uncomfortable. 'There's no need.'

'A courtesy to a visitor,' he said with a smile. 'I am Anders Storstrom, by the way.'

He paused and for a wild moment Gaby wondered whether she was supposed to recognise his name. But then she realised that he was expecting her to give him her own.

'Gabrielle Hyssop,' she said, flustered.

He shook hands with her. 'A great pleasure, Gabrielle. And now we must see. . . Tell me, do you know who is meeting you?'

'No,' said Gaby, looking round.

There were a number of men holding up boards with names. Too late she realised that her chauffeur would have a board labelled Fouquet. Oh, well, it was too late to worry, and probably Mr Storstrom wouldn't notice anyway, she comforted herself. She peered at the names. None was hers.

And then she saw Sven Hedberg. He was in the same dark grey suit that he had worn in London, or one very similar. The austere profile was turned away from her as he scanned the arrivals board. But there was no doubt: the almighty Dr Sven Hedberg in person.

'Hell,' said Gaby under her breath.

Her companion looked down at her.

'There is no one here?' he said, misunderstanding her. 'No problem. I will be delighted to give you a lift to your hotel.'

'I'm not staying in a hotel,' said Gaby absently, her gaze fixed on Sven Hedberg.

'Then you can telephone your hosts from here very easily. Allow me to help you.'

Sven Hedberg had seen her. She saw his eyes find her and her companion. They narrowed with instant displeasure. Even at forty yards she could feel the chill. Why had he insisted on her coming, if he disliked her so much? Gaby thought indignantly. It was his idea after all.

He strode towards her. Taxi drivers and women with innumerable children seemed to melt out of his path. He gave no sign of noticing their existence. For some irrational reason, that annoyed Gaby as much as anything else he had done.

'Thank you,' she said vaguely to Anders Storstrom. 'But here's my. . .' She was going to say gaoler but caught herself in time.

Storstrom looked amused. 'Your. . .?' he repeated quizzically. Then, seeming to realise for the first time that a man was bearing down on them, he stared. 'Good God.'

Hedberg was upon them. 'Good morning, Gabrielle. Are you ready?' he said brusquely.

'Er. . .'

'Good morning, Doctor,' her companion said smoothly. 'Your friend and I were just discussing how

she could contact you.' He held out his hand. 'Anders
Storstrom.'

Sven Hedberg gave him a hard glance. 'I know.' He
didn't shake hands.

Storstrom's hand fell to his side, but he still smiled.
'I'm flattered.'

Hedberg's smile in return was wintry and edged with
danger, Gaby thought, startled. 'I did not intend to
flatter you.'

The other's smile flickered and died. For a moment
Gaby thought she caught a whiff of real dislike. But
then he shrugged.

'We see the world differently, Doctor. You have your
job and I have mine.'

'Inevitably.' Hedberg's voice was hard. 'I just prefer
that you do your job far away from me and my family.'

'I too would prefer that your job did not affect me,'
Storstrom said courteously. 'But we cannot always
choose. Sometimes the circumstances. . .' He spread
his hands.

'I do not make the circumstances.' Hedberg's soft
voice was like an iceberg. 'You do. I heal injuries. You
inflict them.'

Yes, no doubt at all. Real dislike. And it was mutual.
Gaby looked from one to the other, bewildered. There
had to be some personal history here. Such animosity
couldn't be caused by a simple objection to each other's
work. And what did Storstrom do, anyway? He looked
like a businessman, a banker maybe. She wondered
whether she was going to have the courage to ask
Hedberg; and shelved the question temporarily.

'But do you not say in surgery that you have to make
people bleed to cure them?' Storstrom countered.
'Maybe I am doing the same thing.'

'And maybe you are selling newspapers,' Hedberg
said flatly.

'Well, we shall never agree on that.' Storstrom turned
to Gaby. 'It was a great pleasure, Gabrielle. I hope we

shall have the opportunity of meeting again. I wish you a very pleasant stay in Sweden,' he added with an ironic look at Sven.

He took her backpack off his luggage trolley and handed it over with some ceremony.

'Thank you,' said Gaby in a subdued voice. She shook hands rather defiantly. 'You have been very kind. Goodbye.'

Sven watched him walk away from them. Gaby took one look at his set face and judged it sensible to hold her tongue.

'Where did you meet him? Oh, he was on the plane, I suppose.'

To her surprise he didn't sound angry. Instead he sounded as if he was immensely tired all of a sudden.

She said, 'At the airport in London. And then again here. I suppose he could see I was a bit lost. He was kind.'

'I'm sure he was. And you shouldn't have felt lost. I should have been here on time.' Again the weariness. 'It's not your fault. And I should apologise. I was held up unexpectedly.'

Gaby found herself in a quandary. On the one hand, she wanted to say that she had every right to talk to whoever she wanted, and she wasn't accepting his forgiveness for something that wasn't a crime anyway. On the other hand, she was curious. Curiosity won.

'Who is he? A journalist?'

Hedberg looked down at her suddenly, as if really seeing her for the first time since Storstrom walked away from them.

'No. He is a newspaper proprietor.' A look of distaste crossed his face. 'If you call them newspapers. He owns a couple of—shall we say adventurous?—magazines as well. In his own way he is a powerful man.'

Gaby could see that Sven Hedberg was not impressed by Storstrom's power. He seemed to be looking inwards, seeing no very pleasant picture by the look of it. Then he shrugged and looked down at her again.

'No matter. We shall not see Anders Storstrom again. Shall we go? We are already later than I meant.'

To Gaby's embarrassment he bent and hoisted her backpack one-handed on to his shoulder. It looked incongruous against his impeccable suit and tie. She trotted at his side, taking two steps to each long stride.

'Oh, please. You shouldn't be carrying my bag. I'm your employee, after all.'

His eyes glinted down at her in sudden amusement. 'This is an egalitarian country, Gabrielle. The bags are carried by the strongest.'

'But it makes you look ridiculous,' she told him candidly.

He laughed aloud at that. It surprised her. It was a warm, deep sound and astonishingly attractive. He looked younger suddenly, the deep indentations beside his mouth almost disappearing, his eyes alight with laughter.

'That's only because I'm wearing my uniform,' he said. 'I was at the hospital this morning and patients expect it. It seems to give them confidence—God knows why. If I were wearing my normal clothes you wouldn't think twice about it. You should learn not to judge by appearances, Gabrielle Fouquet.'

Gabrielle frowned slightly. Did she judge by appearances? She had never thought so. And what were his normal clothes if the formal, formidable suit was no more than a professional disguise? She found an odd stirring of interest at the thought. Excitement again, she thought. She swallowed hard, trying to give her thoughts a more sensible direction.

They turned out of the airport building before she could say more. He seemed to quicken his pace. Gaby almost had to run to catch up with him. She was fully expecting a luxury Volvo, all electric windows and high performance. But instead he stopped by a high four-

wheel-drive vehicle, the back seat already piled high
with luggage. She saw a couple of mammoth suitcases
and what she at first took to be a television, until she
looked closer and saw that it was the visual-display
screen of a portable computer.

The vehicle itself was dark green, well kept, shiny
and new. But it was not elegant.

He unlocked it and flung her pack on top of the load
in the back seat.

'We're going into the country,' he said drily, at her
look of surprise. 'I don't always stick to metalled roads.
This is the practical answer. Do you object?'

Gaby gave him a cold look, her dislike returning in
full.

'It's up to you how you travel. I've no view on the
merits of different cars, I'm afraid. I usually take a bus.
I would just have expected you to drive something. . .'

'Flashier?' He sounded amused again. 'I've already
told you not to judge by appearances. You seem to be
inordinately hidebound in what you expect of people,
for a girl your age.'

He opened the passenger door and gave her an
entirely unnecessary hoist up into the seat.

'Thank you,' said Gaby, not meaning it.

She shook out the long chestnut mane in a ruffled
manner. He watched her, an odd smile playing about
his mouth. She put her head on one side, enquiringly.
His eyes flickered. Then he shrugged and went round
to the other side.

He swung himself into the driver's seat, closing the
door with a quiet thud that suddenly made the unpre-
possessing vehicle seem a lot more luxurious. He fas-
tened the seatbelt, glanced in the mirror and set them
smoothly into motion. The engine, Gaby noticed, was
also expensively silent.

'How old are you, as a matter of interest?' he asked
casually.

Gaby sent him suspicious look. 'Why?' she said, scenting an insult.

He shrugged, a brief movement of the powerful shoulders that was an insult all on its own.

'Why not?' he asked, concentrating on the path out of the car park.

Gaby couldn't think of a good reason not to tell him.

'Twenty-four,' she said reluctantly.

'Ah.'

He made no other comment. But, looking sideways at the closed, handsome face, Gaby thought she detected that the news was unwelcome to him.

'I'm perfectly competent,' she said, bristling.

He smiled absently, not taking his eyes from the windscreen. That too was a sort of insult; as if she were a child to be indulged with a fraction of an adult's attention. She bristled.

'I assure you. I've done four years of degree work at music college,' she said with bite.

'You astonish me.'

They were through the exit gate. He swung the powerful vehicle round on to a wide road. Just for a moment, Gaby watched the strong, long-fingered hands on the wheel and felt something very strange run up and down her spine.

'Why is that?' Her tone was militant.

'I didn't know there were any music college courses in alternative therapy,' he said blandly.

Gaby ground her teeth. 'I didn't mean in alternative therapy. You must have known I didn't.'

'And yet that's what you're here for,' Sven Hedberg reminded her softly

She was taken aback. 'Of course. But ——'

He interrupted ruthlessly. 'But nothing. That's why you're here. To see if whatever song and dance performance that charlatan has in mind has any effect on my. . .' He stopped, as if he had walked into a wall.

Then he took a deep breath and finished, 'My hand tremor.'

His face was bleak. Unexpectedly Gaby found herself sympathising. Damn that tender heart of hers, she thought viciously. His next words effectively dispelled her sympathy.

'So don't think you're going to charm me into forgetting my action against Hyssop. If this therapy works——' his tone said that he didn't expect it for a moment '—then I will reconsider. But otherwise forget it. The man is utterly dishonest intellectually. He needs to be taught a lesson.'

Gaby bit her lip. The last thing Michael had said to her was, 'Don't forget. Talk him out of legal action, chicken. Even if he loses, Marcia couldn't take the publicity.'

Disconcertingly Sven Hedberg laughed. 'Yes, I thought that was the idea behind all this. It won't work. Stick to the song and dance act, my child.'

His tone said as clearly as if he had put it into words, she thought, that he had no faith in the therapy and no respect for her.

'I'm not a child,' she said, seething.

He looked down at her quickly. 'You certainly did not look like a child in your gypsy costume,' he agreed smoothly.

For some reason, Gaby felt a little cold, clutching sensation just below her heart. She shivered.

'You looked very—worldly.'

She said, 'If that's a polite way of saying I looked tawdry, I agree with you. The point is the management expects you to dress up at In Camera and I can't afford it. So I get my sparkle from Indian scarves I pick up in the market.'

He said softly, 'Why should you think I thought you looked tawdry?'

'Because that's the way you looked at me,' Gaby said frankly.

'Ah,' he said again.

After that they drove in silence for a while. Gaby looked out of the window with interest. They were on a motorway, wide and busy like any other in Europe. The fields on either side were high with crops, golden in the sunshine. Apart from the fact that they were driving on the wrong side of the road, she might just as well have been in rural England, she thought.

Her eyes began to drift shut. Eventually she dozed, and only opened her eyes when she felt the vehicle begin to slow.

'Wake up,' he said, his voice amused. 'Or you're going to miss it.'

'Miss what?' she asked, and then gasped.

They were passing what looked like the largest child's toy horse in the world. Bright red, it towered against a landscape of distant fir trees, dwarfing the vehicles as they passed. It had a cheery geometric pattern round its flanks and a diagrammatic bit and reins. It looked as if it was waiting for some giant's offspring to take it to kindergarten.

'What — is — that?' said Gaby, awed.

'It is a Dala horse.' He sounded amused.

She turned astonished eyes on him. 'A Dala horse. You mean there's more than one?'

'Thousands, probably,' he said blandly.

'Oh, I don't believe that. I'd have heard of them. You couldn't have a country full of bright red fifty-foot-high wooden horses and people not knowing about it.'

He laughed then. 'You're right. This is the only one this big. It is a sign we are entering Dalarna. The decorated wooden horse is very typical of this region. The villagers used to whittle them in the winter, when it was too dark and cold to go out. Then they would take them to market and sell them in the spring. The decoration is very typical.'

They were passing it. Gaby twisted round in her seat to watch it recede in the distance.

'Powerful stuff. I've never seen anything that big that wasn't a statue of a soldier or a politician,' she admitted. 'I like this a lot better, I think. So it's the local emblem of — where did you say?'

'Dalarna.'

He wasn't particularly communicative. He sounded preoccupied. The brief moment of amusement seemed to have passed.

'Is that a town? Is that where we're going?'

'No. And yes.'

Gaby drew an exasperated breath. 'You might answer a civil question,' she muttered.

There was a startled silence. Then to her astonishment he said stiffly, 'I am sorry. I did not mean to be uncivil. Yes, we are going to Dalarna. It is the main lake region of Sweden. I thought my secretary had informed you.'

'She did,' Gaby admitted. 'I just didn't realise that was what it was called.' She sent him a look under her lashes. 'And I didn't understand where exactly we're going either.'

'To my house by the lake.'

She was startled. 'By the *lake*? That sounds pretty rural.'

'It is.'

Gaby was feeling more and more uneasy. 'But it's a village?'

'The nearest village is seven kilometres away.'

She did a quick sum in her head. Maybe an hour's walk depending on the terrain.

'And where's the nearest house?' she said in foreboding.

'In the village,' he replied without interest.

She sat bolt upright, her heart fluttering uneasily under her breastbone.

'Let me get this straight. You're expecting me to stay with you in a house that's an hour's walk from the nearest bar of chocolate?'

'Yes.'

'That's outrageous,' Gaby said firmly.

'That was the deal,' he said equally firmly.

The vehicle sped on at undiminished speed. The full implications of the four-wheel drive began to bear in on Gaby.

'No doubt up an unmade-up track?' she enquired politely.

'In the middle of the forest,' Sven Hedberg confirmed, his voice soft and somehow challenging.

'You didn't think it was worth mentioning at the time when we first discussed this?'

He shrugged. 'I'm paying you a great deal of money. You must have known there would be disadvantages.'

She had thought the fee was extortionate. She bit her lip. 'I wasn't reckoning on solitary confinement,' she snapped.

He slanted a glance down at her. 'It won't be solitary. I shall be there.'

That strange shiver started up her spine again, and the fluttering under her breastbone was almost suffocating. Gaby swallowed hard.

'Solitary would be preferable,' she said tartly, holding on to the appearance of composure at least. 'Did you seriously expect me to put up with it?'

'You were employed to introduce me to the wonders of music therapy, not to go on shopping expeditions for chocolate bars. It didn't occur to me that it would matter.' He sounded impatient again.

Gaby said a little desperately, 'Is there no one else there at all?'

'What are you afraid of?' he said, a taunt in his voice.

They both knew quite well what she was afraid of, Gaby thought indignantly. Any woman in her right mind would be afraid of being shut up in a house in the forest alone with a man who disliked and despised her and turned her spine to melting ice cubes. Especially when he had kissed her nearly insensible the first time they met. That sort of excitement she could do without.

He said softly, 'What are you worried about, Gabrielle? Your reputation?'

'My chocolate intake,' Gaby returned smartly, and untruthfully.

He took his eyes off the road long enough to survey her flushed face and over-bright eyes with considerable comprehension. She thought there might even be a hint of admiration. But he was looking back at the road again before she could be sure.

'We can stock up.' He sounded almost gentle.

'No, we can't. I'm not going to stay,' she announced. Even to herself, she sounded strained and unconvincing.

'Yes, you are.' The husky voice was calm. 'You need the money.'

'Not that much.'

'Oh, I don't think a struggling musician could afford to repay me the fare and compensate me for the loss of valuable time, to say nothing of reneging on a contract,' he pointed out.

Repay the fare? But Michael had paid her fare. Hadn't he?

'And you insisted on first class, I hear.'

Gaby said, 'I thought my——' She remembered that Sven Hedberg did not know that she was Michael Hyssop's daughter. In the circumstances it was probably just as well that he remained in ignorance. 'I mean, I thought Michael was paying my fare.'

'And he sends you everywhere first class?' His eyes brushed over her briefly. 'It is understandable, I suppose. So why doesn't he buy you a dress to play the piano in?'

There was more than a hint of cynicism in the cool voice. Gaby sat up very straight.

'He probably would if I asked him.'

'So why do you not ask him?' He was mocking her.

Gaby was faintly bewildered. 'What has that got to do with you?' she challenged him.

He laughed. 'You are quite right, of course. It has nothing to do with me how you conduct your private life. I should not have asked. Tell me instead what you know of Anders Storstrom.'

Gaby was even more bewildered. 'Nothing. I'd never met the man until today. I've never even heard of him.'

'No? And yet he owns many titles in the States. As I'm sure your —— ' He broke off, artistically echoing her own former hesitation. 'Michael Hyssop could tell you.'

Gaby flushed. She did not pretend to misunderstand him. 'I know you're angry about the piece in the magazine but it was a mistake. Honestly.'

'It was indeed,' he agreed. 'And someone is going to pay for it. So are you going to stay or not?'

Gaby bit her lip. She thought of the unknown Marcia and her two fatherless children. Once again there was no choice, she found. She sighed.

'I'll come quietly,' she said.

CHAPTER THREE

THE journey seemed to go on forever. Sven Hedberg appeared to be tireless. Long after Gaby was beginning to wilt, he drove on with an easy mastery that didn't disguise his unflagging concentration on the road. They left the motorway and the other cars on the road thinned out.

Gaby watched the scenery in a daze. He took them through orderly farmland, past lakes, glimpsed through the trees at the side of the road, across a flat stretch of country with marshes in the distance, birds wheeling and calling above them.

He spoke very little. Occasionally he would point something out, a mining town in the distance, an old wooden church in a village they went through, but all his concentration was for his driving.

In the circumstances that was just as well. Gaby had a nasty feeling that she had walked up to the edge of a chasm. She was wondering whether she had quite the sophistication required to spend a month alone with a man like Sven Hedberg without making an almighty fool of herself.

She stole a look at him. What sort of man was he really? She knew he was distinguished in his profession because her father had told her so. She presumed he was rich, given the shocking figure he was paying for a course of therapy he did not even believe in.

But what sort of man was he personally? She could see for herself that he was powerfully attractive in an icy way. He did not attract her, she assured herself. That excitement was all too obviously mixed with fear. She was fascinated by him. Just as she might be fascinated by a strange and dangerous animal. But that was not attraction. At the thought of another of those heart-stopping kisses, Gaby almost shuddered.

No, she could not find him attractive. He was too cold and unforgiving of her father; too cold and combative to herself.

Yet what, after all, did she know of him? Perhaps the house by the lake would tell her, she thought. People put a lot of themselves into their homes. She must see what she could detect from it.

But when they arrived she forgot everything else, in sheer alarm.

The house wasn't by the lake. It was in the middle of it. They crossed a rickety wooden bridge with Gaby sitting bolt upright, one hand clenched on the edge of her seat, out of sight.

'Don't be scared.' Sven sounded faintly amused. 'This bridge has stood for thirty years.'

'Then maybe it's time it was replaced,' she muttered.

He laughed. 'It's repaired regularly. You have to take care of things if you live in the wilderness.'

Gaby gave a little shudder. It had been over an hour since they had seen another house. The village, she deduced, must be further on, if it were only seven kilometres away.

'Why do you?' she asked, more to take her eyes off the lake water that was all too close to the vehicle than because she had thought about the question.

'Live in the wilderness?' He shrugged. 'I don't. This is the family summer house. We have had it for generations. We always spent the three summer months here when I was a boy.'

They were out in the middle of the bridge and it seemed to Gaby to be creaking alarmingly.

'Do you share it with the rest of your family?' she asked rapidly, shutting her eyes.

She had the impression that he tensed. But all he said was, 'There is only me now.'

The car seemed to take on a little spurt. The bridge creaked louder. And then they were on the other side.

Sven opened the door and swung lightly down on to the grass. Gaby made haste to follow before he could come round to help her to alight. She had not forgotten the odd sensation of his hands on her when he had put her into the vehicle. She was not courting a recurrence.

She looked about her. They were standing in front of a white-painted two-storey house that looked big enough for any number of families. Facing them Gaby counted six windows on each floor. They were currently covered by wooden shutters, which gave the house an oddly sinister, blinded air, under its steeply sloping roof. It looked like an old man who frowned all the time. She shivered a little, though the sun was blazing.

Sven, she found, was not looking at the house. He was shading his eyes, looking across the lake. She followed his gaze but could see nothing. She went over to him.

'What can I do?'

He turned to look at her. His expression was enough to make her exclaim involuntarily, 'What's wrong?'

He seemed to recollect himself. His usual remote expression closed down over the handsome features. 'Nothing. Let's go inside. You can make coffee and I'll get the car unpacked.'

He produced an old key, quite six inches long, and led the way to the door. It was a big wooden affair. It swung open reluctantly, it seemed to Gaby, with a grinding of protesting hinges.

'Oil hinges,' said Sven Hedberg, committing it to memory. 'This way.'

Once he had thrown open the shutters, the kitchen was a great airy room with two windows, looking out at the lake. Gaby exclaimed in delight.

'We cook on a log-fired stove here. It gives us hot water as well. Until that gets going, though, you'll have to use the little calor gas stove.'

Gaby's heart sank — not at the implication that she would be doing the cooking. She liked cooking. But she had hoped that there would be a housekeeper of some sort, to protect her from the danger of Sven Hedberg's exclusive company. And the limitations on power was another problem.

'No electricity? What about my tapes? What about my synthesizer? How am I going to play them? How am I going to follow a therapy programme?' Her voice rose.

'Maybe you'll have to sing to me instead,' he said coolly.

She looked at the closed, handsome face and realised, with a little shock, that he was laughing.

'There *is* electricity. You're winding me up,' she said in resignation.

'I'm afraid so,' he agreed. 'The power lines tend to come down in storms; that's why we don't use it to cook or heat. But in the summer months it's quite reliable. You should be able to play your magic chants without losing power.'

Gaby refrained from reminding him that her magic chants seemed to be, by his own account, his last chance.

Instead she busied herself with making coffee in a great cast-iron pot that she found. There were coffee beans, smelling wonderfully fresh, and an ancient grinder. No instant coffee, she saw ruefully.

Sven unpacked the car with a speed and efficiency which meant that he had emptied the loaded car by the time the coffee had filtered. Gaby heard him running up and down the uncarpeted wooden stairs as if he were carrying no load at all, although the cases in the back had looked substantial. He had already discarded his jacket in the car but as soon as he had taken his suitcases to his room he changed rapidly into jeans and an open-necked shirt.

Gaby did a double take when he came into the

kitchen. He seemed to have shed twenty years with his suit. The immaculate hair was rumpled from his exertions and he was smiling. In the sunlight, the grey wings at his temples almost disappeared. His hair glowed like copper, flopping casually over one eye so that he looked like a boy. He looked more approachable than she had ever imagined he could.

Paradoxically his conversion to informality made her feel suddenly shy.

'Coffee smells wonderful,' he said.

Gaby found herself looking away. 'I couldn't reach the mugs.'

He laughed. 'No, you're a little thing, aren't you? In spite of those long legs.' He reached the mugs down from the shelf above the sink. 'We must remember to leave them accessible for you. I'll tell Barbro.'

Gaby was pouring coffee. 'Barbro?'

He accepted his mug, looking momentarily rueful. 'I wasn't entirely frank when I said we'd be alone here. There is a lady from the village who comes in. Most of the time she is just a caretaker to an empty house, of course. But when I'm here she will cook and clean up a bit. I'm usually working and haven't got time for things like that.'

Gaby wondered briefly whether he would ever, in any circumstances, have time for household chores. But she kept it to herself.

'Will she come in today?'

'She's been.'

Gaby was startled. 'But there's no food. . .'

'I bring it down with me. There's a box in the hall. Barbro only stocks up for me as I run out. She has her own family to care for, after all.'

This was unexpected consideration from imperious Sven Hedberg. Her face must have shown her reaction because he laughed out loud.

'I told you, little Gabrielle, don't judge by appearances. I'm as capable as the next man of remembering how heavy shopping can be.'

Gaby wasn't at all sure she liked being called 'little Gabrielle'. It made her feel like a puppet in his hands.

'I'm not a child,' she flashed. She remembered too late that it was the second time she had said that.

His lips twitched. 'I'm counting on it.'

She glared at him.

'I haven't got time to watch out for a child,' he explained blandly. 'I've got work to do.'

She subsided, blushing faintly though she had no idea why. But she said, 'I thought you were here to relax and get your health back.' Though even as she said it she looked at the muscles in his arms where they rippled under the cotton shirt and realised that was nonsense. And she remembered the personal computer in the car.

His face closed again. Really, she thought, he was the most difficult man.

'I'm perfectly well. I just have an occasional motor tremor which I need to get rid of. It doesn't interfere with my thought processes. I have a paper to write. It must be with the *Medical Journal* in three weeks.'

'Oh,' said Gaby, thinking of fitting the relaxation sessions round the schedule of a man with a deadline. What slim chance she had ever had of success seemed to be receding by the minute.

'And I have case-notes to review.' He didn't sound as if it was open to negotiation. 'I work in my study. When I am there I am not to be disturbed. It is the room opposite this.'

'And what am I supposed to do while you're poring over your computer?' Gaby demanded.

His lip curled. 'There is the lake. It is safe for swimming. There is a small beach further along the shore. I will show you. Or you can go for walks. There are no nature trails here, so you will have to be careful. But as long as you take a compass you should be safe enough.'

Gaby, a town girl, looked at him in horror.

'A *compass*?'

'So you can find your way back to the house,' he said reasonably. 'If you go somewhere where the tree cover is dense it may be difficult to locate the direction of the sun.'

She did not say that being able to locate the sun would be unlikely to help her in any event. She did not need to.

'Unfortunately I was never a Boy Scout,' she said acidly.

He gave her a cool look. 'Unfortunate indeed. It might have taught you self-discipline.'

Gaby was still choking on the insult when he said briskly, 'Come along. I will show you the rest of the house.'

Gaby followed him perforce. All the floors were wooden, most of them exquisitely polished. There were beautiful and, she suspected, valuable rugs in every room, sometimes several. They creaked, however.

'You know where anyone is in this house,' she observed, wincing as one of the stairs groaned louder than most. 'Not much chance of a private life here.'

'There is not much chance of a private life whenever you permit yourself to share a home with anyone,' he said unexpectedly.

Gaby stared. 'That's a sweeping statement for a scientist,' she observed. 'How many experiments have you made?'

He stopped and looked down at her, his eyes glinting. 'If that's an oblique way of asking me whether I'm emotionally committed, the answer is no.'

'It isn't,' said Gaby, startled and annoyed.

'In fact we may as well get that cleared up right from the start,' Sven went on, unheeding. 'As Michael Hyssop so cleverly pointed out to the American Press, I have relationships with women. Some have been purely social, some — less so.'

'Less pure?' said Gaby sweetly. 'Or less social?'

The icy grey eyes gleamed appreciatively. 'Both.'

'Fascinating,' she said in a bored voice.

Sven Hedberg laughed. She had the feeling he was not deceived by her mask of indifference.

'The women in my life,' he said deliberately, 'are well aware of the rules.'

Gaby nodded. 'Your rules,' she said. It was not a question.

He shrugged. 'The rules of common sense. No commitment, no pain. The basis of the relationship is agreed from the start, of course. I don't mislead anyone.'

Gaby wondered what it would be like to be one of the lovers he had not misled when Sven decided the time had come to part. Not nice, she thought.

She said curiously, 'And you've never wanted anything else yourself? Never?'

'No.' He sounded very certain. 'And I cannot believe that at my age I shall change. So if you have any ideas, bear that in mind.'

'Any ideas?' Gaby stared at him. Then suddenly she realised what he meant and she flushed. 'You're crazy,' she said shortly.

His mouth twisted. 'You are young and attractive and you've already got the idea that this place will bore you. No matter what your arrangements are in London, I will be the only man available for the next month. And we are alone. It would not be so very surprising.'

'Yes, it would,' said Gaby firmly.

Quite suddenly she was remembering Tim's seeking hands and her own horrified freezing. She shuddered. No, she was no risk to Sven Hedberg, or any other man for that matter.

'It's not a game I play,' she told him. 'Your rules or anyone else's. Anyway, I don't like you.'

He was not offended. For a moment he even looked unforgivably amused. 'If you have not yet learned that dislike is not necessarily a bar to sexual attraction, you are even younger than I thought.'

Gaby was not going to let him talk down to her. She looked him straight in the eye and said levelly, 'Attraction is one thing. Doing something about it is another thing entirely.'

His eyebrows rose as if she had surprised him.

To clinch it she said, 'And in case *you* get any ideas, Dr Hedberg, let me make it plain that I don't sleep with men I work with.'

The fact that she didn't sleep with any men at all, thought Gaby, was something that she was keeping strictly to herself.

To her surprise he laughed again, that warm, throaty chuckle which was so damned attractive.

'Very wise. I'll bear it in mind.'

'Do that,' she said in an encouraging tone. She felt rather pleased with herself. She seemed to be handling this unpredictable sophisticate very adequately. 'Now, where's my room?'

He gave her a long look, as if she puzzled him. Then he shrugged quickly and led the way down a dark polished corridor.

'Apart from the staircase, all the windows are in the rooms,' he said. 'So the internal passages are dark. That's why we leave these everywhere.'

He indicated a narrow table set against the white-painted wall. It was a beautiful piece of furniture, painted and stencilled with a design of leaves. On it was a small serviceable chamber light, containing a white candle and a box of matches in the saucer.

'For when the electricity goes off,' he explained, switching on the overhead light.

'I'll remember.'

He took her to the end of the passage and stopped.

'Your room,' he said, indicating a plain door. 'The bathroom is next door. I hope you will find everything you need.' He hesitated. Then he said deliberately, 'I am on the other side of the staircase. At the end of the corridor.'

In other words, thought Gaby, as far away from her as he could get. It should have been comforting. But somehow it suddenly made her feel — exiled.

'Thank you,' she murmured, flushing.

She thought he looked at her with a good deal of understanding.

He said gently, 'Anyone can be alarmed in a strange house. You must feel you can come to me if you need anything.' His mouth twisted a little. 'I won't misinterpret the signs, I promise you.'

That made Gaby feel worse.

'I thought I wasn't supposed to interrupt you,' she said, rallying.

'Not when I'm working, no. My study is out of bounds. I must not be interrupted. Unless there's an emergency, I suppose,' he added as an afterthought.

He didn't sound very sure about that, thought Gaby.

'But you don't mind being interrupted when you're asleep?' she asked curiously.

The handsome face closed again. 'I don't sleep much. And I sleep very lightly. If you knock I will hear you.'

'You're very kind. But I won't need to disturb you,' Gaby said, devoutly hoping it was true. 'I'm not nervous and strange houses don't worry me.'

She hoped the last would prove to be true too. Normally she fitted in easily, whenever she stayed somewhere new. But there was something about this brooding, blinded house that kept her looking over her shoulder. In spite of the polished wood that gleamed where the sun struck it; in spite of the dazzling white paint on the walls inside and out; in spite of the pretty furniture and the rich rugs; in spite of it all, there was something dark here. Gaby shivered.

Sven evidently saw it.

'Well, don't be too proud to change your mind, if you feel uneasy. You wouldn't be the first person to be uncomfortable in this house.' His face darkened. Gaby thought he was looking inwards and the memory was no very happy one. But then he shrugged, throwing it off. 'I will leave you to unpack. I shall be in the kitchen if you want me.'

He turned and left. Gaby watched him. How tall he seemed in the narrow confines of the corridor. Tall and somehow isolated, as if he carried his own vacuum around with him and nothing quite touched him. As if he was the loneliest man in the world.

She shook herself. What was she thinking of? It must be tiredness after the journey. She was not normally so fanciful.

She pushed the thought away and went into her room. After the muted electric light of the corridor, it was dazzling. Gaby actually put her hand up to shade her eyes.

Sven had put her backpack at the foot of a large wooden double bed. Someone, presumably Sven also, had thrown back the shutters. There were three large windows, one on one wall, two on the wall at right angles to it. The room was ablaze with sunshine. It turned the white-painted cupboards to snow and ice. It turned the Bokhara rug to jet and ruby. And it turned the pine bed to liquid gold.

Gaby sat down with a little thump on the nearest chair. It was like being on stage, she thought, remembering the heat of spotlights during recitals. She couldn't imagine a greater contrast to the rather grim feel of the rest of the house.

Suddenly she began to smile. She stretched in the warmth of the sun, feeling it on her face like a caress, as if she were sunbathing in the open air.

There are going to be compensations, she told herself. She stretched her arms above her head luxuriously. Big compensations.

She realised she was tired. It had been an early flight and the long hours in the car since then had added to her sense of cramped weariness. She looked longingly at the bed. He obviously expected her to go back to the kitchen as soon as she had unpacked and freshened up. But surely a small snooze wouldn't hurt?

The bed was covered with a heavy crocheted counter-pane. Gaby drew it back carefully — and met a surprise.

Although the bed had the usual complement of duvet and pillows that the most exacting guest could require, it had no linen on any of them. She stripped back the duvet and turned over the pillows, searching. To no avail. Not a sheet or a pillowcase in sight.

So guests made up their own beds on arrival in this house. Well, it might not be very hospitable but it wasn't the end of the world. Gaby began to hunt the room for sheets.

After turning out every drawer and cupboard — and making some surprising discoveries in the process — she had to admit defeat. She had found some wonderful Edwardian lace gloves, a positive library of photograph albums, and an elegant chased-silver set of brushes and hand-mirror. But no sheets and pillowcases.

She would have to ask Sven. It was a small defeat in its way. She had so hoped to prove that she was capable of looking after herself in his house without flying to him for support every ten seconds. But at this point she had to admit herself defeated.

As she expected she found him in the kitchen. He was loading food out of an ice-packed container into the freezer. He looked up when she came in.

'I've failed your first initiative test,' Gaby announced.

His eyebrows flew up. 'Can't find the bathroom?'

She thought she detected scorn. It made her wince. 'Can't find the sheets for my bed,' she admitted.

He straightened, closing the freezer door. 'But. . .'

'I've looked everywhere I could think of in my room. I didn't fancy scouring the house.'

'Of course not.' He was frowning. 'Your room should have been prepared. I——'

There was a clatter followed by the sound of falling machinery. Gaby jumped. But Sven was quite undismayed.

'Here is Barbro now. She will be able to explain.'

He strode to the front door and went outside. Gaby followed him.

An unexpected sight met her eyes. Sven was helping a tall, thin woman untangle herself from an ancient bicycle. A newspaper and several letters were scattered on the grass. Gaby picked them up.

Sven and the woman were engaged in a rapid conversation in their own language. The woman sounded agitated and faintly indignant. But Sven, Gaby saw, was amused.

At last he propped the bicycle against the wall of the house and turned to her.

'I'm afraid you have every right to complain,' he said ruefully. 'Barbro assumed you would be sharing my room during your stay. I forgot to explain the circumstances of your stay here. I apologise.' His eyes glinted down at the lady bicyclist. 'To both of you.'

Barbro sniffed loudly. She had an ugly, angular face and very shrewd blue eyes.

'Yes, you should. You've embarrassed me and embarrassed your guest.' She strode over to Gaby and shook hands with a bone-crushing grip. 'I'm sorry. He never explains, this one. And usually. . .' Her bright, angry glance at Sven made it perfectly clear that usually her assumption would have been perfectly justified. 'I thought I was wasting my time, coming up to see if everything was all right. It's just as well I did.'

Sven held up his hands in a gesture of amused surrender.

Gaby said shyly, 'It really doesn't matter. If you'll just tell me where the sheets are. . .'

Barbro sniffed again. 'I suppose *this* one didn't know.' She sent him another bright, angry glance. 'Oh,

go away and research something,' she said sharply. 'I'll
make up the bed.'

To Gaby's astonishment he laughed and went inside.
This left her confronting the angry, angular lady.
Admittedly she didn't seem to be angry with Gaby at
the moment but it was still a disconcerting experience.

Abruptly the lined face broke into a broad smile.

'No need to look so scared, child. Sven's a wild one
but he doesn't cheat.'

A *wild* one? Gaby thought of the impeccable suits
and the clipped, controlled manner.

'He doesn't seem very wild to me,' she said
involuntarily.

The sharp blue eyes narrowed. 'That's when he's at
his worst. You need to keep your wits about you when
he's pretending to be respectable,' Barbro said unexpectedly. 'How long have you known him?'

'I don't,' said Gaby, startled. 'That is, we've only just
met. I —— ' She hesitated. He had hated her father
telling the world that he was using alternative therapy.
Maybe she shouldn't mention it either. So she said
uncomfortably, 'I'm doing a job for him.'

Barbro's eyes searched her face. Then she shrugged.
'You know your own business best. But don't ever
forget he's dangerous. Now let's find those sheets.'

Gaby's bed was made in an efficient couple of minutes, with Barbro talking all the time. She seemed to
know the whole family well. And for some reason she
was bent on giving Gaby a full briefing.

'This was the family summer house from the end of
the last century. They were always rich. Sven and
Elisabeth used to come here every summer from the
time they were born.'

'Elisabeth?'

'His sister,' Barbro said, punching the duvet vigor-
ously into shape.

'I see. Do they share it?'

'She's dead,' Barbro said abruptly, pulling up the crocheted cover.

It was somehow shocking in the brilliantly sunny room.

'Dead?'

'Nine years ago. It was an accident.' Her lips thinned. 'At least, that's what they called it.'

Gaby felt uncomfortable. She had the feeling that Barbro had not intended to pass that particular comment on to her. It had just bubbled up from some deep feeling somewhere. It was clear that the woman was deeply attached to Sven, for all her strictures.

Gaby wondered what Sven's sister's death might be called if it wasn't an accident; and didn't know how to ask; or even whether she really wanted to know.

Barbro smoothed the counterpane lovingly. 'She had a difficult life, Elisabeth. She and Sven both did. Erik was crazy about their mother and she—well, Kristin was a law unto herself always. Erik thought it was the children that bored her. That's why he was so strict with them. They mustn't make a noise, mustn't be rough. . . He thought that it was the children who drove Kristin into running off all round the world. But she would have done it anyway. She was—what is the word in English? Reckless. Yes, that's it. She wanted adventure. She wanted to try new things. She always came back to him. But it wasn't enough for Erik. He wanted her with him all the time. But no one could tie Kristin down. It made Erik very bitter.'

She looked out of the window and added deliberately, 'Sven gets it from her. Can't stay in one place. Won't stay faithful to one woman.'

Gaby realised she was being given information for her own good.

'Look,' she said gently, 'it's very kind of you but you really needn't worry. 'I'm here to do a job. Nothing else. He may be Don Juan of the twentieth century, but it doesn't make any difference to me.'

Barbro's sharp eyes scrutinised her.

'You ever been in love?' she asked sharply.

'Well — no. . .'

'Got a boyfriend? A steady date?'

'I go out with lots of men,' Gaby said defensively. 'But most of the time I'm working. My career is at a critical stage. I haven't got a lot of time for socialising.'

Barbro gave her a look that could only be described as pitying.

'And you think you're safe from Sven Hedberg?'

'Yes, I do,' said Gaby hotly.

'You're wrong.' It wasn't unkindly said but it was a flat contradiction.

Gaby flushed. She could see that the woman meant kindly but it infuriated her that everyone kept talking to her as if she were an inexperienced child.

'I am twenty-four, you know,' she said.

'Ripe for it,' said Barbro cynically. She sat down suddenly on an embroidered footstool under one of the long windows.

'Listen to me, child. I've known Sven Hedberg all his life. He's been taking any woman he wants since he was seventeen. Even women who know what he's like. He's like a magician, mesmerising his victim. I don't understand it.' She thought about that for a moment. 'Well, yes, I suppose I do. While he's hunting, he's all charm. The poor creature thinks she's the only thing in the world he's interested in and cares about. Then he loses interest and. . .' she spread her hands expressively '. . .tragedy. He's always been the same. He — isn't kind to women who love him.'

'I don't,' snapped Gaby. 'So I should be safe, don't you think?'

Barbro hugged her knees. 'Not if he wants you. I tell you, child, he's dangerous. Look after yourself.'

'Why should he want me?'

Barbro laughed.

'I mean it,' Gaby said, flushing. 'If he wanted a

girlfriend here, he could have brought anyone. There
are hundreds of candidates from what you say. I'm a
stranger. He doesn't even like me.' Any more than I
like him, she added under her breath, though she was
not saying that to an evident long-standing friend. 'Why
do you think he should be interested in me?'

Barbro looked up at her, her head on one side.

'You really don't know?'

All of a sudden, Gaby heard the unwelcome echo of
Sven Hedberg himself saying 'dislike is not necessarily
a bar to sexual attraction'. She shivered suddenly.

But she said, 'No. It sounds pure fairy-tale to me.'

Barbro stood up abruptly. 'And what if I told you
Sven didn't just forget to tell me you were coming here
to work? That he didn't tell me deliberately? What if I
tell you he told me to make up one bed and one bed
only? His bed,' she added for good measure.

Gaby stared at her in dismay.

'I don't believe it.'

Barbro shrugged. 'Suit yourself.'

'But—why should he bother?'

The other woman shrugged again. 'If you had to be
here anyway to help him with his research, maybe he
thought it was an agreeable way of passing the time.
Or—' She looked at Gaby searchingly. 'Had you
made him angry?'

Gaby thought. 'I suppose I had,' she said at last. 'Or
at least an associate of mine had. And then he—Sven
and I—we seem to annoy each other.'

'There you are, then,' said Barbro triumphantly.

'You're saying Sven would try to seduce me for some
sort of revenge? To score a point off me? That's
ridiculous.'

Barbro's eyes clouded. 'Maybe he wouldn't,' she said
with a sigh. She didn't sound very convinced. 'I don't
know how well I know him any more. When he was
younger he had more scruples. But he's got harder as
he's got older. And some of the women who have been

here were as tough as he is.' She bit her lip. 'Don't get me wrong. He's a good man. An honourable man. It's just in this one area that he seems to think he can do what he wants and it doesn't matter who gets hurt.'

'That's — terrible,' Gaby said slowly.

Barbro nodded. 'If I were a psychiatrist I'd probably say he was revenging himself on all women because his mother left them. But —'

'But?' prompted Gaby.

'I suspect it's simpler than that,' Barbro said sadly. 'He doesn't respect women because he's never had any reason to. And he does exactly what he wants with them because he's always been able to get away with it.'

There was a small silence. Gaby felt chilled. She found Barbro was watching her as if she expected some response. In the circumstances there was only one thing she could say.

'Not with me, he won't,' Gaby vowed.

CHAPTER FOUR

BARBRO left soon after that. Sven was already in his study, working. Gaby unpacked her tapes and synthesizer and then considered supper.

Sven emerged pushing a hand through his red hair in an absent fashion. The hand was trembling slightly, Gaby noted. She did not say so.

Instead she said in a neutral voice, 'I could do scrambled eggs.'

Sven looked startled. Gaby observed it with interest. Not much sign of the cold-blooded seducer there, she thought, no matter what Barbro thought. It was a relief.

'Forgotten I was here?' she enquired.

He was shaken by a silent laugh. 'Completely,' he admitted. 'You don't make much noise, do you?'

'Wait till you hear me practising Rachmaninov,' Gaby said darkly. 'Even on a synthesizer I can shake the rafters.'

He sat down at the kitchen table and looked at her with open amusement.

'Rachmaninov on a synthesizer? Isn't that heresy for a pianist?'

'Absolutely,' Gaby agreed. 'It's fun, though. What about scrambled eggs?'

He ran his hand through his hair again. It made him look younger and distinctly rakish. And alarmingly attractive. Maybe it would be worth bearing Barbro's strictures in mind, even if she did not entirely believe them, Gaby thought.

'Fine,' he said. 'Whatever.' He grimaced. 'I didn't mean to leave you to cook tonight. I just started looking at a case and forgot the time.'

'It's all right,' she said, surprised. 'It's not late.'

Sven laughed. 'It's ten-thirty,' he said.

'*What*?' Gaby did not believe him. She looked at her watch. Sure enough it was half-past ten. She looked at the gentle grey light over the lake, like an English twilight, and shook her head. Then she remembered her geography and could have kicked herself.

'Land of the midnight sun, right?'

'That's Lapland. We're not quite that far north. But we are a lot further north than Stockholm. And it's nearly midsummer. The nights are short.'

Gaby looked out of the window again.

'I never realised,' she said, marvelling.

Sven stood up and came to stand beside her. She was very conscious of him at her shoulder as she looked out at the silvery landscape.

'It's a very special time for us,' he said softly. 'So much of the year it is dark and cold here. At midsummer we can go a little mad.'

He seemed to have forgotten her again, Gaby thought as he fell silent. Yet she was conscious of the warmth of his body like a fire at her back. She drew an uneven breath.

'Mad?'

He leaned forward to look down the lake, cupping one long-fingered hand round her upper arm as he did so. Gaby tensed at the casual touch. Sven did not notice.

'Behave out of character.'

She looked up at him, startled. The harsh lines on his face had smoothed out in laughter. Laughter, she realised suddenly, that he was willing to share with her.

'Sober matrons swim naked in the lake by moonlight,' he said in thrilling accents. 'Fathers of families fight over basketball like their own sons. Aldermen dance.'

Gaby choked. 'Awesome. And all because the nights are short?'

The grey eyes were as silver as the landscape.

'Short and precious,' said Sven Hedberg softly.

Suddenly he was not laughing any more. Neither was she. The stillness in the simple room was absolute.

Oh, my lord. Barbro was right after all. You have got to watch out. The thought came to Gaby abruptly.

She whisked away from that light touch on her arm.

'Eggs,' she said breathlessly.

He let her go without resistance. Gaby thought she caught an ironic gleam, though. She ignored it.

She prepared the simple meal with merciful efficiency. Privately she was relieved. She had been afraid that, with unfamiliar pans on an unfamiliar stove, her limited skill would let her down.

'Excellent,' Sven said when they had finished. 'Thank you.'

'Think nothing of it,' Gaby said airily. Then, honesty overcoming her, she laughed. 'Well, at least I didn't burn them. Or something equally bad for the ego.'

He was amused. 'Why should you?'

'Because you make me nervous,' Gaby said frankly.

His mouth slanted. 'I know.'

She was startled; and slightly affronted.

'What do you mean, you know?'

Sven leaned back in the bentwood chair and stuck his thumbs in the belt of his jeans.

'Don't forget I kissed you,' he reminded her.

Gaby jumped. She had not forgotten exactly. But she had managed to put it out of her mind. Though it was still there, like a wild animal trying to sneak into a tidy domestic house when the door was left unguarded.

She said through a constriction in her throat, 'I thought I wasn't to get any ideas?' She sounded cool and self-possessed, she realised with some surprise. She did not feel cool and self-possessed. 'Surely it's better to forget about that unfortunate episode?'

The handsome face wore a curious expression. 'Can you forget it, Gabrielle?'

She made a quick gesture, rejecting the query.

'That's not a fair question.'

He raised an eyebrow. 'Why do women always cry unfair when a man asks an honest question?' he asked cynically. 'All I want is an honest answer.'

Gaby glared at him, her previous antagonism surfacing with alarming promptness.

'No, you don't,' she contradicted. 'You want me to say no, I can't forget that you kissed me. And then I'm supposed to fall palpitating into your arms, I suppose.' Her voice was full of scorn.

Sven's lips twitched. 'Not palpitating,' he murmured.

'Well, yes, I remember it,' Gaby flung at him, ignoring the interruption. 'With a great deal of embarrassment, to be truthful. If I'd had my wits about me I would have taken your head off.' She sounded unmistakably wistful.

Sven shook his head. 'You're very bloodthirsty. It was only a simple kiss.'

'It was a calculated insult,' Gaby said coldly.

He considered that, his head on one side. 'Would you call it calculated? I thought it was pretty spontaneous myself.'

Gaby all but stamped her foot.

'On both sides,' he added.

There was enough truth in that to give her pause. Sven watched her, interested.

'You took me by surprise,' she said at last, carefully.

He chuckled. 'I took us both by surprise.'

'What do you mean?' She was suspicious.

His mouth slanted. 'My rules say no strangers,' he said coolly. 'It only leads to complications.'

Gaby was outraged. 'It—you—if you mean what I think you mean. . .'

'I do.'

'Then you were seriously deluding yourself,' she informed him. 'I was never a candidate to play games with you. Rules or no rules.'

'I know.' He shook his head as if something puzzled him. 'The last person in the world I imagined being attracted to was Michael Hyssop's — assistant.'

The hesitation was an insult all on its own. Gaby stared, a thought dawning that had not occurred to her before. She opened her mouth to ask him but Sven was still musing.

'And you weren't looking for anyone else either, were you? In fact, I'd say that you were running scared on a number of counts.'

Gaby closed her mouth with a snap. She was disconcerted. How had he deduced that? Was it just disappointed vanity? She had not immediately melted at his feet, so there had to be something wrong with her. A lucky guess? Or had that shocking kiss really told him something about her? Something that nobody else seemed to have noticed in three years?

'Hyssop, I suppose, is no threat,' he added.

Gaby stood very still. So she was right. He thought she was involved with Michael. He could not know they were father and daughter, of course, because Michael had very carefully concealed it.

She should tell him the truth, Gaby thought. There should be honesty between therapist and patient, if for no other reason. She knew perfectly well that she should tell him. She also knew she was not going to. She was not at all sure why.

Sven said softly, 'You're a creature of secrets, aren't you?'

She jumped. Was he reading her mind? Gaby did not like the idea at all. It strengthened her resolve not to tell him one damn thing more about herself than she had to. Especially as she was certain there were things he was keeping to himself. Else why had he started blocking the treatment as Michael had described?

'That makes us equal, then.'

'You think I have secrets?'

She narrowed her eyes at him. 'Are you saying you don't?'

There was a sizzling pause. Then Sven turned away. 'You must be tired.'

It was his formal tone again. Somehow the abrupt way he had broken off the intimate exchange was as shocking as if he had suddenly shouted at her. Gaby almost physically recoiled.

'You should go to bed.' It was an order.

'Very well,' said Gaby, making it plain that she recognised it as such.

He did not turn. 'You know your way?'

'Even to the bathroom,' she agreed acidly.

He did turn then. He gave her a polite smile that did not touch his eyes. 'Sleep well.'

For a shivery moment she wondered whether he was going to repeat his invitation to call on him if she felt nervous in the strange house. But he didn't. He was as remote as the high mountains she had glimpsed beyond the lake.

'Goodnight,' she said quietly.

He was right about the tiredness, she realised. She was so tired she forget to close the shutters. So at six o'clock the light of a Scandinavian summer morning was beaming into her eyes. She fought to stay asleep for twenty minutes or so. Then she gave up.

She pulled on cut-off jeans and a T-shirt and went downstairs. The front door stood open. Slightly alarmed, she went to it.

But then she saw that there was no reason for alarm. Sven was up before her. He was standing in the middle of the bridge looking out across the lake. Gaby stood very quiet, watching.

The lake was so calm, it looked like a piece of jagged-edged glass dropped by a giant. She could see the tall pines, the distant hills and the sky in a reflection without a flicker of movement. A bird flew out of the trees, calling. She saw it in the water, crossing the lake in a graceful, curving flight.

Sven saw it too. She saw him look up, his attention caught. Against the clear morning sky, his profile was painfully handsome.

It wasn't that he didn't still look arrogant, she thought. Of course he did. With that high-bridged nose and sculpted, scornful mouth he was always going to look arrogant. But the arrogance matched the sweep of the landscape.

There was nothing gentle or cosy about the forested slopes or the peaks that towered behind them, and even the lake looked bottomless and mysterious as if there was a whole world beneath the surface. For all its calm and beauty it was a dangerous landscape. Not one she would lightly enter on her own. One where she could feel herself lost and overwhelmed by the very beauty of the quiet lake.

She looked at Sven Hedberg again. Barbro had called him dangerous. At the time Gaby had interpreted that as meaning that he was a sexual predator. That he would try to seduce an unimportant passing lady guest if it amused him. That he wouldn't care if she got hurt.

But looking at the man in his natural landscape she suddenly felt that he could be dangerous at a deeper and more elemental level. As if the laws of the city and civilisation didn't apply to him. As if he was somehow part of this uncompromising country. As if the most important part of him was a great secret, drowned but still waiting, way, way below the smooth and shining surface he showed the world.

Gaby clutched her arms in front of herself in a quick defensive movement.

His stillness was absolute.

She found herself holding her breath.

Then, quite suddenly, he turned and ran lithely back across the bridge. As he came closer, their eyes met. Gaby realised that he had heard her.

'I'm sorry,' she said. 'I didn't mean to disturb you.'

This morning his eyes were the intense grey of storm clouds; not icy at all. She blinked at the intensity.

'You didn't.'

She watched the beautiful mouth shape the words and thought that if she only had the ability to hear it he was speaking at a different level. The ability, Gaby thought suddenly, or the will? Did she really want to know his secrets, after all? No sensible woman walked into danger. And she was very sensible — while she had the strongest feeling that this man's secrets could be dangerous.

She said hurriedly, 'We ought to talk about the therapy. When would suit you?'

He gave her an ironic look. 'I thought the therapist was in control? Shouldn't you decide?'

'You're thinking of orthodox medicine,' Gaby retorted, almost glad to be sparring with him again after those odd few minutes. 'That's the one where you, the patient, hand yourself over and let the scientists do what they want with you.'

The look of irony deepened. 'You've read the witch doctor's manifesto, then. Even if you're only a musician.'

Gaby let that pass. 'If you're not going to co-operate,' she said with heat, 'we'll get nowhere. I might just as well go home now.'

He laughed then. That husky laugh that sent little aftershocks up her spine.

'I'll co-operate. Do you want breakfast or does it work best on an empty stomach?'

Gaby looked at him. 'It works best when you're relaxed,' she said candidly. 'When did you last relax?'

For a moment he looked startled. Then he shrugged.

'I've always got up early.'

She thought of the way he had looked on the bridge; the absolute stillness of leashed power, like an avalanche waiting to happen.

'And you don't sleep much. After you've driven all day without stopping,' she said in a scolding voice.

He looked amused. 'I've got a lot of energy.'

'Evidently.' Gaby pushed back her long tumble of hair. 'Look,' she said earnestly, 'you need to stop if this therapy is going to be any use. I mean really stop. Not just pause. Not give me an hour before you go back to your computer. Or even two hours.'

He looked at her. Then he said irrelevantly, 'Do you always wear your hair like that?'

Gaby jumped, disconcerted. 'Like what?'

He hesitated. 'Loose,' he said in that husky voice.

It had that effect on her senses with which she was becoming familiar. She ignored it determinedly.

'Does it matter?' she asked, feigning impatience.

He was insistent. 'Do you?'

'Actually no, as a matter of fact,' she said with something of a snap. 'I've only just got up and I haven't had time. . .' Her voice trailed away at the look in his eyes.

She remembered that she was alone with Sven Hedberg in the middle of a lake in the middle of a foreign country. She drew a shaky breath.

He must have seen her expression change. At once he turned away. The warmth died out of his face, the stark lines beside the beautiful mouth becoming suddenly apparent. He looked, thought Gaby, chilled, as if he was ice at heart, no matter how charming he sometimes chose to be.

'You'll need to pin it up when you light the gas,' he said coolly. 'It's a danger near a naked flame.'

'I—I usually plait it,' said Gaby. She had an odd feeling that she had been reprieved.

'That would be safer. While you are here I would prefer it.'

Gaby didn't make even a token bid for independence on the matter.

'V-very well,' she said in a subdued voice.

'And on the matter of the therapy I am sure you are right. We will start after breakfast. You shall have as much of my time as you want.'

'Need,' Gaby corrected swiftly.

His smile was twisted. 'Need. Of course.'

She had said something wrong. She didn't know what. She looked at him hesitantly. He gave her one of his wintry smiles.

'Go and plait your hair, little Gabrielle. I will make breakfast.'

She went, biting her lip.

But when she came down again a few minutes later, his mood had changed entirely. He was polite and, if not exactly charming, friendly enough in a neutral way. He had prepared an excellent breakfast of soft rolls, ham and cheese slices, too. Gaby concluded that he just didn't like being disturbed in his early morning meditations.

He certainly made no more slighting references to music therapy. He even showed a certain interest as she set up her portable synthesizer and unobtrusively consulted her mother's notes.

'You need to lie flat at first,' she instructed. 'You tense every muscle in your body, starting with your feet, and hold the tension while I play.' She demonstrated. 'Then you let it go when I do this.' She played a crashing chord that made him blink. 'Got that?'

'It is not difficult,' he said gravely. 'I think I can manage it.'

He flung himself down unselfconsciously. He moved like a mountain animal. Gaby found herself admiring the long, graceful limbs and turned swiftly back to her instrument, a little shocked. She didn't normally look at men's bodies like that.

She twiddled an unnecessary knob or two, swallowing. 'Ready?' she asked in a constrained voice.

'Whenever you are.'

Devoutly hoping he had not detected her confusion,

she began to play. The trick was to make the difference between the two styles of playing smaller and smaller, so that in the end the patient was responding to the music, rather than the shock of the loud relaxation chord.

Sven Hedberg, she saw, responded almost at once. So he was probably musical. The trouble was that his relaxation was only superficial. The fact that she had suspected as much wasn't much comfort to Gaby. Helping people relax who had spent years resisting it was, as she knew from her mother, a lifetime's work.

At the end of the exercise she kept her hands on the keys. If she could, she wanted to keep him in harmony with the sounds.

'Now stand up,' she said softly, in time with long, languid arpeggios, 'and sit in the big chair. Close your eyes.'

His expression was wry. But he followed her instructions without objection. He didn't move like a man who had just had a relaxation exercise, Gaby saw. Her heart sank another few inches.

He tipped his head back and shut his eyes. He had a long throat. The strong column was tanned. He looked as if he had spent hours in the open air, she thought suddenly.

'Look at our eyelids,' she said, dropping her voice. 'At first you see only red. Then you start to see a landscape.' She moved into Chopin, not so familiar that he would recognise it, not so obscure that he would not have heard it before. It had a feeling of lake water, she realised. 'Trees. A great sky. The lake. . .'

To her astonishment, his whole body jerked. His eyes flew open.

'Clever,' he said in a voice cracking ice.

Gaby's hands fell with a crash on to the keyboard. She gaped at him.

'Did Michael Hyssop send you here to spy on me?' he said in a harsh whisper that came close to hatred.

'And introduce you to Anders Storstrom so you know where to send your discoveries?'

Gaby began to feel as if she was in a nightmare. She saw the cold fury in his face and didn't know what she'd done to put it there.

'I — don't understand. . .'

'Did Barbro tell you?'

She stared at him, moistening suddenly dry lips.

'Tell me what?'

He stood up. He looked immensely tall. The expression in his eyes was terrifying.

'That my sister died in the lake. That I failed to get her out in time.'

Gaby flinched. 'I — I had no idea,' she protested, distressed.

'No?'

'No.' She searched her memory. She had been so tired last night that she had only taken in half of what Barbro had said, she knew. But surely she would have remembered something as dreadful as that?

'She said your sister died in an accident,' she said slowly.

She was remembering something else. She was remembering Barbro adding obscurely, 'At least that's what they called it.'

His eyes raked her face. She felt as if she was being X-rayed. She lifted her chin. 'I don't tell lies,' she said quietly.

He expelled a slow breath. The anger visibly drained out of him. 'No. I can see you didn't know. I shouldn't have accused you.'

Gaby turned off the synthesizer. The atmosphere for relaxation therapy had clearly gone. She turned her back on the synthesizer and leaned forward, looking at her hands.

'Where did it happen?'

For a moment she thought he wasn't going to answer. Then he shrugged.

'Here.'

He said no more. After a pause Gaby said gently, 'Is it so deep, then, the lake?'

Sven looked at her impatiently. 'Yes, it is, as it happens, but it wasn't that. She could swim like a fish. It doesn't have to be deep to kill. You can drown in three inches of water if. . .' He stopped.

What had he been going to say? If someone holds you down? If you want to die?

'How did it happen?'

In an uncharacteristic movement he pushed his hands through his hair. Even on the bridge this morning the fox-red thatch had looked controlled. Now it was disarranged, with a lock falling forward over his brow. It made him look like a pirate on the quarterdeck.

'It was stupid,' he said curtly. 'We had a small boat then. She took it out on the lake. We have some bad storms. One blew up. She couldn't manage the boat on her own. It overturned.'

Gaby didn't speak. It was clearly not the whole of the story. It might also be all he was willing to tell her. She held her breath.

At last he said, 'I had been climbing. I was coming back on the lake path. I saw the boat capsize. I saw someone in the water. I went in. But—I was tired. I'd been climbing rocks all day. The water was rough. I couldn't get to her.'

Gaby was appalled. She could imagine it so easily: the rain and wind and the heaving water, with Sven watching her go down before his eyes, unable to reach her. Was this his secret? No wonder he wanted to keep it suppressed, she thought. This was far worse than what Tim had done to her and yet she had never been able to share that with anyone.

'It must have been terrible.' She was holding back tears.

He shook his shoulders suddenly, as if he were throwing it off. 'It was nine years ago.' He sent her an acute glance. 'And no, before you ask, I don't blame myself.'

Gaby jumped. It was exactly what she had been thinking. In fact she had been telling herself that here was the source of the tremor in his hands; repressed guilt could be a powerful physical influence, she had learned from Anne.

He said wearily, 'I'm a doctor, Gabrielle. The one thing you learn to live with as a doctor is chance. Sometimes it works with you. A patient recovers against all the odds. You give thanks to God. But sometimes chance goes against you. If a doctor blamed himself every time that happened, he'd go mad. This was the same. It was an accident. I did my best. Chance went against me.'

He didn't, she noticed, say that chance went against Elisabeth. Gaby looked down at her hands. She felt very young and untried suddenly.

'Nothing like that's ever happened to me. I don't know whether I could cope with it,' she said honestly.

'You'd cope.' It was quiet.

She looked up, startled. 'How can you say that? How can you know?'

Sven seemed to hesitate. Then he shrugged. 'People do. And I'd say you're as resourceful as they come.'

She was oddly disturbed by the compliment. Don't overestimate me, she wanted to say. Don't treat me as if I'm your equal in experience.

'I don't know what you base that on. You hardly know me.'

His eyes glinted in the way she had come to recognise. It meant he was about to score a point.

'Quite. And already you've got me talking about subjects I don't normally discuss with my closest friends. Wouldn't you say that was resourceful?'

She was taken aback.

'And I've hardly been kind to you.' He didn't, she observed, express any regrets about that. 'I've been

rude and overbearing. And I've seen you bridle. You
didn't like it. But you've hung on in there and now
you've got me telling you about the darkest time of my
life.' He was dispassionate. 'Resourceful hardly covers
it. Witch, maybe.'

Gaby was under no illusions that it was intended as a
compliment. In spite of the coolly reflective tone, she
had a sense of real anger in him. She didn't understand
the reason for it. But she didn't think it was going to
make her summer's task any easier.

She hesitated. At last she said carefully, 'Isn't that
what you're paying me for?'

The handsome mouth twisted.

'A diplomat too. A witch and a diplomat to boot.
That's a dangerous combination.' He looked at her
broodingly.

Gaby felt a tremor of nervousness. She quelled it.
She took hold of herself, her chin lifting.

'I don't see how I could possibly represent any danger
to you.'

The brooding look didn't lift. But the thin, sensual
mouth tilted. 'Don't you?' he murmured.

Gaby shook her head. 'No, I don't. It's ridiculous.
But if you don't want me here, you have only to tell me
to go.'

Her eyes met his. His expression was quite unreadable. There was a silence like the space between
lightning and the thunderclap.

At last he said softly, 'Yes, I can do that.'

'Well, are you going to?'

She could detect no expression at all in the level
gaze.

'Not just at the moment,' he said slowly.

Gaby found she had been holding her breath. Which
was ridiculous. It didn't matter to her whether he told
her to go or stay. Did it?

She'd never believed in her ability to talk him out of
suing Michael anyway. And as for helping him over-

come his hand tremor — well, he didn't believe there
was much of a chance that she could and neither, in her
heart of hearts, did she. So she'd be better off out of
here. She'd be better off back in civilisation where
there were people and shops and the soothing bustle of
everyday life. Where she didn't feel hopelessly out of
her depth.

'You want me to stay?' she said. Her doubts were
showing, Gaby thought. He would notice that.

Sven's eyes flickered. He didn't answer directly.

'An experiment,' he said. He gave an abrupt laugh.
It sounded harsh to Gaby. She winced. 'For both of us,'
he concluded.

He must have seen the unease in her face. He turned
away abruptly.

'You don't feel comfortable with me,' he said over
his shoulder in a cool, professional tone. 'That's going
to get in the way.'

Gaby gave a shaken little laugh. 'Isn't it me who
should be saying that?' she said ruefully.

Sven turned back to her. His eyes glinted suddenly.
'Ah, but I have more experience in these relationships.'
His tone was bland but Gaby knew perfectly well that
he was mocking her.

She flushed. She did not ask which relationships he
was referring to. She was pretty certain she knew.

His tone gentled. 'We really know very little about
each other. Wouldn't it be easier if we were to talk this
morning? Just talk? We could go for a walk and you
could tell me about yourself.'

Gaby looked at him doubtfully. 'Do you talk about
yourself to the patients you treat?' she challenged.

His mouth twisted again. 'But I only treat the disease,
not the whole man,' he countered.

Gaby gave up. She'd heard her mother say a thou-
sand times that that was the weakness of orthodox
medicine. She'd never expected to have the argument
turned against her as a weapon. But then she'd never

expected to argue with a master of the art like Sven Hedberg either.

She stood up, sighing. 'Very well.'

It was full sun outside. The house had no formal garden but the ground around it was filled with a tumble of lilac and clumps of wild lupin. There was a grassy stretch between the house and the shore. As they walked through it, Gaby detected buttercups and speedwell in great splashes of colour among the waving grasses.

'It's beautiful,' she said involuntarily.

Sven shrugged. 'It is untouched. In the autumn I scythe this year's growth, that's all. I plant nothing. And I don't try to keep anything alive that wants to die.'

Gaby shivered suddenly, in spite of the heat of the sun.

'That sounds bleak.'

'It is the natural law. I don't pervert it.'

She stared at him. 'But—you're a doctor. Your whole profession is perverting the natural law. You save people who would die without you.'

He looked down at her. 'People are not plants,' he said. 'They don't always know when their time is over.' His voice was unemotional. 'But mostly my work is not so dramatic. It is helping people to live without pain or the restrictions their condition would otherwise impose.'

Gaby was impressed. He sounded like a good doctor, she thought. One her mother would admire, in spite of his slighting reference to alternative therapists as witch doctors.

She wondered suddenly how badly his tremor affected his work. She said, 'Your hand—does it stop you working?'

Sven looked down at it, turning it over. There was no tremor now, Gaby saw.

'Working? No. Operating? Sometimes. I can't work

for as long as I used to. And it's not always reliable if I'm tired.' He shrugged. 'Nothing to make a fuss about.'

Except, thought Gaby with sudden perception, he would hate not being in control of his own body, not knowing when the hand was going to let him down.

'How did it happen?' she asked gently.

He put his hands in his pockets. His casual shirt was half open to reveal the strong, tanned column of his throat and a glimpse of equally tanned chest. The red hair, already disarranged, lifted softly in the slight breeze off the lake. He looked very relaxed and casual.

But his voice wasn't casual. It was cool and precise and utterly devoid of feeling.

'I was sailing with a friend in the Baltic. There was an old ferry going to Riga. The crew was new, though. The master didn't know the waters and he didn't keep far enough out from shore. He holed her on a submerged rock. She sank. My friend and I helped.'

Gaby was thoughtful. 'You got a whole ferry crew on to a small sailing boat?'

'It wasn't a large ferry,' he said drily. 'The whole crew was only eight. But no, of course you are right. And there were passengers too.'

'Did your own boat sink?'

'No.'

He was not very informative. Gaby knew he didn't want to talk about it. Yet somehow she felt it was important that she knew what happened.

'So how did you manage?'

He made an impatient gesture. 'We radioed for help, of course. And Leif ferried people to land and came back.'

It didn't sound desperately taxing, or even very dangerous, the way he described it. Yet Michael had said he was too long in the water and that was the start of his hand tremor. Gaby frowned.

'How long did all this take?'

He shrugged. 'There was fog. The rescue boats had

trouble finding us. It took maybe six hours to get everyone back to shore.'

She was horrified. 'And you were in the water all that time?'

'Yes.' He was curt. He clearly found it painful to remember, Gaby thought.

'Was anyone—hurt?'

His voice was even. 'Everyone survived on that occasion, if that's what you mean.'

On that occasion?

Then suddenly she saw, in a blinding revelation that had her wondering how she could have missed it before. It was not the ferry rescue that troubled him so badly. It was the other occasion, nine years earlier, when he had failed to rescue his sister.

She said carefully, 'What did the hospital say about your hand? I mean, you must have been in shock.'

'It was nothing,' he said almost savagely. 'Nothing at all. I am fit and it was a warm night. There was no shock. There should have been no after-effects at all.'

She was right. He hated his weakness.

'So why the tremor?' Gaby asked.

He expelled an explosive breath as if he was letting all the anger out of him.

'Who knows? Medicine is such an inexact science. That's why I thought. . .'

'The one per cent chance?' Gaby said gently. 'I understand.'

He gave her a brooding look.

'I think perhaps you do,' he said slowly. He did not, she thought later, sound very happy about it.

CHAPTER FIVE

SVEN retired to his study all afternoon. Gaby heard the occasional bleep from the computer. It was usually followed by a curse that she was grateful she did not understand.

She took her mother's notes out into the sunshine and applied herself to them. Eventually she slept.

It was a particularly fierce bleep and virulent curse that brought her awake. She came out of her dream with a heart-stopping lurch. She had been dancing soundlessly with a tall masked man through a forest and he had suddenly let her fall into a pit she had not seen.

Gaby sat up, not sure where she was, one hand pressed to her galloping heart. Then another expletive brought her back to reality. She grinned and stood up, brushing down her jeans.

She went over to the open window of the study. She hesitated, remembering that Sven had warned her not to interrupt him. But when he looked up, he did not appear to see her as an interruption.

'Defeated by a computer?' asked Gaby, much entertained.

Sven looked at the screen with dislike. 'It's got nothing to do with the computer. There must be thunder in the air. The current keeps surging. I forgot to bring my surge suppressor with me. I've just lost an hour's work.'

'If you've only just lost it, you'll remember it,' Gaby comforted him. 'You just need to write it down quickly.'

He transferred the dislike from the machine to her.

'A consoling thought. I'll do that. Thank you.'

Gaby laughed. 'I'll make some coffee.'

He came out into the kitchen while the percolator was bubbling. His hair was wild and he had an ink stain on one cheek. Gaby fought an urge to wet a finger and rub it off.

'Given up?'

'On the computer certainly.' He looked out of the window. Clouds were beginning to drift over the horizon. 'There it is,' he said. 'Storm coming unless I'm much mistaken. That computer is off until the thunder has passed. I'm not risking losing any more.'

The coffee was ready. Gaby poured it into two mugs and gave him one.

'Which language do you write in?' she asked curiously. 'Your English is so good that sometimes I forget it's not your own language. Barbro's was the same.'

Sven laughed. 'When you come from a country of eight and a half million people you can't afford to be chauvinist. Everybody in Sweden speaks at least one other language fluently. Usually more than one. When I'm writing hospital notes or letters to patients, I use Swedish. Everything else is in English or German. Mainly English. The major research is in the States. And the Japanese speak it.'

Gaby nodded. She had played with a Japanese string quartet and had been amazed by their mastery of English.

'Do you travel a lot?'

His smile was lop-sided. 'All the time.'

'Do you enjoy it?' she asked.

He shrugged. 'What's to enjoy? You've stayed in one Intercontinental, you've stayed in them all. You don't meet local people. You meet the other figures in your own field, whom you already know. All that changes is the scenery and the price of Scotch.'

It sounded bleak. Gaby sipped her coffee, watching him. She had never heard of a life which sounded so lonely, she thought.

'Is that why you're so determined not to get involved?' she blurted.

'Involved? You mean with women?' The handsome face was cynical. 'Oh, I've been involved with women.'

Gaby fought down a blush. 'I don't think you and I mean quite the same thing by involvement,' she said drily.

His eyes narrowed. 'Judging from what I saw between you and Hyssóp, we mean exactly the same thing,' Sven remarked in a dispassionate voice.

Gaby stared. Then the full meaning of what he had said broke in upon her. For a heartbeat Gaby was so angry that she could have thrown her coffee over his cynical, handsome face. Then, perversely, she decided to let him believe that she was every bit as decadent as he thought she was.

So she lowered her lashes, regarding him from beneath their curling shadow. She said airily, 'Oh, that's different.'

He raised sceptical eyebrows. 'In what way?'

Gaby spread her hands. 'Well, he understands me very well.'

'You mean he knows that older men can't be choosers. That you're out for what you can get and he has to learn to live with it,' Sven translated with irony.

Gaby blinked. There was a real bitterness there. She stopped pretending to be a *femme fatale* and said curiously, 'What makes you say that?'

'I told you. I've been involved with a lot of women,' Sven said cynically. 'Before I formulated my own rules, I got burned like every other young fool.' He leaned his elbows on the table and looked deep into her eyes. 'Men and women don't really like each other, you know. They make bargains because the biological imperative means they need each other. But the bargain is based on mutual mistrust. Downright hostility sometimes.'

The biological imperative! Gaby was chilled. She drew back a little.

'I don't believe that.'

He shrugged. 'Believe it or not, it's the truth.'

She searched his face, troubled. 'What's made you like this, Sven? Your mother?'

The lines in his face deepened. The red hair flopped forward. He pushed it back with long fingers. For some reason, watching the movement of that elegant hand made her mouth go dry.

Excitement, thought Gaby again. Physical excitement. In spite of the cynicism of what he was saying; in spite of the fact that he was obviously ice at heart, he made her feel more physically alive than anyone had ever done. She recognised the sensation. But how on earth had it crept up on her this time?

He looked wicked and deeply uncaring. Ice at heart indeed.

'Who told you about my mother?' he said indifferently. 'Oh, Barbro, I suppose. Well, yes, if you want to know how I formed my view of women, Kristin undoubtedly contributed. But so did my sister, my first lover, my secretary and a long, long line of colleagues and colleagues' wives.' His mouth slanted upwards in a cruel smile. 'To say nothing of subsequent lovers. The only thing that women have in common, my dear Gabrielle, is that they all want something from men that men don't want to give.'

She wanted to smooth that harsh smile away from his mouth, too. She wanted to kiss him. The thought shook her.

'*You* don't want to give,' Gaby corrected tartly.

She found his cynical exposition oddly painful, she realised. But she was not going to admit that either. What was it that this man did to her?

'If you lay down all the rules and then tell your women they're only out for what they can get, I'm not surprised you've been burned,' she told him, repressing

the thought energetically. 'I'm only surprised you
haven't been murdered.'

He gave a sudden crack of laughter.

'You're very frank.'

Gaby gave him a cool look.

'Why shouldn't I be?'

He narrowed his eyes at her so that he was looking
calculated and wicked again.

'You are here all alone, after all. In my power. What
if I decided to teach you a lesson?'

Instinctively she gave a small shiver at the suggestion.
To her chagrin it was not entirely one of alarm.

'What sort of lesson?'

That glittering, slanting smile was back. He folded
his arms across her chest and eyed her speculatively.

'Shall we say — not to talk to strangers?'

'Oh, I've learned that one,' Gaby said drily. 'Or kiss
them either.'

There was a glint in the grey eyes. 'You kissed
Anders Storstrom?' he asked, politely interested.

She choked. 'Yes, of course I did,' she retorted. 'I
just flung myself upon him in the first-class lounge until
he begged for mercy. What is it about this man
Storstrom?'

His eyes flickered. Then he shrugged. 'Once, long
ago, he and his paper destroyed something I — would
have been able to save. We have watched each other
very carefully ever since.'

Gaby bit her lip. Suddenly she was beginning to
realise why he had reacted so strongly to the innocuous
paragraph about him in the Hollywood magazine.

'The Press are destructive?'

'And liars,' he agreed. 'Encouraged by people like
Hyssop.'

There was more than a grain of truth in that. Michael
liked his publicity. Even though he had not briefed the
journalist on Sven's consultation, Gaby recognised that
Marcia would never have done what she did if she

hadn't known that Michael valued publicity. Her brow creased.

'For example,' Sven said softly, 'you may recall that little piece of nonsense in LA coupled my name with that of Oriana Meadows. I had dined with her once. They would have more justification for saying that you and I are in the middle of a torrid affair. At least we are living together.'

All of a sudden Gaby felt as if she was being suffocated.

'We are not,' she said through stiff lips, 'living together.'

'Oh, but we are. I intended that we should.' He was smiling. But he was quite implacable.

She shook her head. 'Because of what the papers said about you in LA? As some sort of revenge on Michael? You're crazy.'

'My motives,' Sven said suavely, 'are best described as mixed. But the opportunity to demonstrate to Hyssop the pain caused by an inaccurate Press report is undoubtedly a bonus.'

He smiled at her but there was something relentless about the pleasant expression all the same. Gaby felt cold all of a sudden.

'I won't put up with it,' she told him, trying to calm her inner trepidation. 'I'll leave.'

'You can try.'

There was amusement in the casual voice. She peered up at him, trying to gauge the reason for that private laughter.

'What do you mean?'

'You won't find the key to the Land Rover easily,' he said, reaching casually for his coffee.

'There must be taxis. I've got enough money.'

He flashed a look down at her. 'First catch your taxi.'

'I know there's a village,' Gaby told him, not without triumph. 'I'll ring for a cab to take me back to Stockholm.'

'You've found a telephone?'

Her eyes widened. She passed what she had seen of the house under feverish review. No telephone.

'I'll walk to the village, then' she said. Did he think she was so weak-minded that she wouldn't find a way to get away from him?

The village wasn't that far either. What was it Sven had said? Seven kilometres?

A muscle twitched in the handsome face. Again she had that unpleasant sensation that he was laughing at her.

'You know how to get there?' he asked courteously.

She started. They hadn't passed through a village on yesterday's journey. She had thought at the time that it was because it must lie in the opposite direction from Stockholm. Now she wondered whether Sven hadn't taken a deliberate detour, so that she should not know in which direction to walk.

She said slowly, 'I shall ask Barbro. I'll go back with her.'

'That would have been a good plan,' he agreed. 'If Barbro had been coming back.'

Gaby stared.

'I took the opportunity to tell her yesterday night that she needn't bother with the house any more. Not as long as we're here,' he explained blandly. 'I'll take care of whatever shopping we need. You can do the housework. She wants to concentrate on rehearsing for the midsummer festival. She was relieved.'

Gaby felt her heart lurch. She had not realised how much she'd been relying on Barbro's comfortable, commonplace presence.

Now she looked out of the window at the empty landscape. You could get lost in those trees and no one would find you for days. The sky was darkening rapidly. Below it the lake was beginning to stir like a huge animal awaking.

Gaby swallowed. Suddenly it was no longer peaceful

and secluded. Instead it began to look like a wilderness, vast and threatening. Her eyes went round the opposite shore. Trees bordered it, so thickly planted that they looked almost black. She couldn't detect a single break in the line that might indicate a path.

You could be imprisoned here as efficiently as in a building with iron bars, Gaby thought. She looked at Sven, interpreting that private laughter at last.

'You've thought of everything, haven't you?' she said quietly.

'I believe so.'

She shook her head. 'And do you think I'm going to let you get away with it?'

He looked faintly astonished.

'What else can you do?'

And that was the galling thing, Gaby thought then, and later. There wasn't a thing she could do about it. The quiet forest, the beautiful lake were effectively her gaolers. Sven Hedberg was playing games with her and there was not one damned thing she could do about it.

He drained his coffee-cup and put it back on the table. 'I must get back to work,' he said. He touched one long finger to the corner of her mouth. Gaby held her breath. But he was laughing.

'Don't look so worried. I'm sure you'll be able to convince Hyssop it was all perfectly innocent. If you want to, that is.'

And, laughing softly, he closed the door on her.

Left alone with the thunder clouds gathering outside, Gaby wandered round the house, wondering what he expected her to do with herself. Clearly he wanted no interruptions. Did that mean she couldn't play? Slightly to her surprise she found a fine Bechstein in the formal salon. It needed tuning a little but Gaby had played on bargain-basement instruments and had no difficulty with providing first aid.

She sat down and tuned it carefully, one eye on the door. She half expected Sven to come bursting in, demanding that she stop the instrusive noise. But he didn't. And if he didn't mind the awful monotones of tuning, Gaby argued to herself drily, then he couldn't seriously object if she practised properly.

So when she finished, she ran her hands over the keys experimentally. They had the slight resistance of an instrument that wasn't used to being played.

'Never mind, my beauty,' Gaby crooned softly. 'We'll soon play you in.'

She didn't know how long she had been playing when a strange feeling made her look up. Sven was standing in the door watching her.

Gaby jumped. Her hands fell on to the keys in a startled discord. His expression was unreadable. But for some reason her heart fluttered in her throat.

She caught herself. She was not going to let him intimidate her any more. If her playing disturbed his concentration, he had no one but himself to blame. She wasn't going to apologise. She lifted her chin and stared back at him.

At last he moved, strolling into the room. He crossed the polished floor silent-footed and leaned against the piano. Gaby watched him warily. She wasn't going to be the first to speak, she promised herself.

He ran a hand over the dark wood, looking down at the keys. The bitter lines on his face were suddenly marked.

'This hasn't been played for years,' he said.

'I can tell.'

'Yes, I suppose you would.' His tone was absent.

He was frowning. Gaby thought he was absorbed in memories. She wasn't even sure that he remembered she was there.

'Who played?' she asked quietly. 'You?'

'The whole family. Once. When we were still pretending we were a family.'

The grey eyes were hooded. Gaby sat very still. All her defensiveness dissolved in sudden concentration.

He wasn't meaning to tell her this, she thought. But it was important. She knew it was important.

'When was that?' she prompted at last. She said it very softly, so as not to jolt him out of his reverie.

But he sent her a sudden, narrow-eyed look. She had lost him, she realised; lost the mood and the unguarded, unedited memories. She bit her lip.

'Clever,' he said in an entirely different voice. 'Did Hyssop provide you with a list of questions? Or is that Storstrom's influence?'

Gaby sat up very straight. There was something in that look, in that voice, that sent a cold trickle down her spine. Her heart began to thud somewhere up in her throat.

'I do not know Anders Storstrom,' she said with precision. 'I had never met him before he showed me where to find a telephone at Stockholm airport.'

But Sven was not listening.

'You don't miss a trick, do you?' he went on, in that soft, deadly voice.

She moistened her suddenly dry lips. 'I don't know what you mean.'

'Oh, I think you do.' His eyes were icy.

Gaby shook her head.

'Get the victim talking,' he went on, watching her, his eyes opaque. 'Get him so he forgets whom he's talking to. Then sell it all back to him at the end of the session as all your own work.'

Gaby swallowed. 'That's not fair.'

His smile was mirthless. 'Isn't it? But I spent a lot of time watching Hyssop, you know. I recognise the technique.'

She felt a distinct tremor of apprehension. But she said with spirit, 'Are you seriously trying to tell me you'd forgotten who you were talking to just now?'

His eyes flashed with such anger that her head went back as if at a physical blow. At once the steep lids veiled their expression.

'No,' he said levelly. 'No, I wouldn't say I'd forgotten you.' He began to stroll round the piano. 'But wasn't I supposed to?'

Gaby edged away along the length of the piano stool. 'No, of course not. I ——'

'Saw an opportunity and seized it,' he supplied mockingly. 'Hyssop would be proud of you.'

Gaby thought of what her father would say if he knew how inadequately she had handled Sven Hedberg up to now. She grimaced.

'I doubt it,' she said wryly.

Sven was as quick as a cat. 'Because you haven't got me dancing to your tune? Keep on trying, darling. Maybe you'll manage it.'

He was just a step away from her now. If he put out a hand he could touch her. Gaby came to her feet in a movement she didn't even have to think about.

'Don't touch me.'

His eyebrows flew up as if she had really astonished him. His eyes narrowed. 'Are you afraid of me?' Sven asked softly as if she had surprised him.

Her head reared up at that. 'I'm not afraid of anyone,' Gaby told him.

'Then you're a fool.' His tone was contemptuous but the cold, intense eyes were scanning her expression like lasers. 'There are some people it makes sense to be afraid of. And some situations.'

She put a hand to her throat to ease her constricted breathing. Was this one of those situations? Did he mean her to think it was? She was not going to give him the satisfaction of seeing he disturbed her, she vowed.

'Are you threatening me?' she flung at him.

Again that look of surprise, quickly masked. 'I? Why should I do that?'

'You're dangerous,' she muttered, remembering what Barbro had said — and what she had felt herself in his overpowering presence.

He dismissed that with a flick of a long-fingered hand.

'All men are dangerous given enough provocation, my little gypsy. You must have found that out for yourself without my help.'

Gypsy? Oh, he must be referring to the clothes she wore to play in the restaurant. They made her look deceptively sophisticated, Gaby remembered, her heart sinking.

'But I haven't provoked you,' she pointed out, trying to maintain a reasonable tone.

'Haven't you?' It was soft, even meditative, but there was a question in the cool grey eyes that she found she could not meet.

Gaby dropped her eyes hastily. 'I —'

His hands closed on her shoulders. She went very still.

'So you think I'm dangerous,' he mused. 'But you're not afraid of anyone or anything.' He held her a little away from him, looking down at her. 'And you don't think that constitutes provocation?' There was an undercurrent of laughter in his voice all of a sudden.

She swallowed. 'Why should it?'

'You don't think that could be something of a challenge?' he suggested.

Through the thin T-shirt his hands felt amazingly warm. And strong. Gaby tried to ignore it.

'A challenge?' she echoed faintly.

'Inviting me to do my worst,' he explained.

She could feel the warmth of his whole body. Was she suddenly nearer to him? Had those hard hands been drawing her imperceptibly closer?

Her head began to whirl. 'You want me to be afraid of you?' she croaked.

'Afraid? No, of course not.' He sounded impatient. 'A little respect would be nice,' he added softly with a laughing, wicked look that made Gaby's blood run suddenly cold.

The strong hands tightened. She caught her breath as if he were hurting her. Which he wasn't. At least not physically. As his mouth touched hers, her eyes were tight shut and a small prayer wheel was going round and round in her head: This man is not Tim Nation; it will be all right. He's not Tim; it will be all right.

His kiss was hard. Gaby shuddered under it. His hands moved. Through the light material they forced a burning trail of sensation on her consciousness.

Respect? She was terrified, Gaby thought. She knew why, too, and it was only partly to do with the forest fire he was spreading through her veins. *He's not Tim*, she reminded herself fiercely.

The kiss gentled. One hand went to cradle her head. He began to coax her silently, his every move a seduction.

'Open your mouth,' he murmured.

It was impossible to shake her head.

'No,' said Gaby.

Which of course accomplished what he wanted.

It was not a forest fire, it was a conflagration, sudden and total. All thoughts of Tim and three years of careful celibacy were sent whirling out of her head. All thoughts of anything melted into incoherence. She was all sensation. Sensation she had never felt before.

Her hands lay against his chest, frail as butterflies. Her whole body lay against his, powered by his warmth, engulfed by his passion. When he raised his head, she was wide-eyed and helpless, clinging to him as to the only stable object in a reeling world.

'Well,' he said in an odd voice.

He brushed a stray drift of hair from her face. For a moment Gaby wondered whether his hand was entirely steady. Then she realised the position she was still in. With a little gasp, she levered herself out of his arms, her face flaming.

'Is that how you usually go about getting respect?' she flung at him.

He looked at her, a small smile curving the handsome mouth. Something in the smile infuriated her. She stepped back and, almost without realising it, raised her hand. Sven caught her wrist in mid-air.

'No,' he said quietly. 'I don't choose to let you hit me simply because you don't like what you've just found out.'

Gaby's breathing was hurried. 'I already knew you were a rat. I haven't found out anything new.'

One long finger traced the line of her cheekbone. It felt almost like tenderness. Which had to be an illusion. But for a moment it felt so gentle she could have cried. Gaby closed her eyes briefly.

'Oh, I think you have,' said that soft, confident voice. 'I think we both have, for that matter.'

She opened her eyes. 'You delude yourself.'

'No.' The grey eyes were very steady.

Gaby turned away abruptly. Now that there was a space between their bodies, she found she was trembling imperceptibly. It infuriated her. No man had the right to make her tremble. No man.

'I'm not scared of you,' she said fiercely, as much to herself as to Sven.

His eyebrows twitched together. 'I never thought you were.'

He surveyed her. She was clasping her hands tensely together. She wouldn't meet his eyes

'Or not until now.' He paused. 'What's wrong, Gabrielle?'

She lifted her head. 'Sex isn't in the deal,' she said brutally. 'I'm not here as your light entertainment for the month.'

He froze. His face became the mocking mask that she was used to. There was a silence. Gaby swallowed. Then he said softly, 'Now there we agree.'

Before she had any idea of what he intended, the strong hands had closed round her wrists. He jerked her back into his arms without any pretence of seduction. His mouth was insolent on her skin. There was none of that illusory tenderness this time either. He was simply a sophisticated man that she had, unwisely, managed to make very angry. And he thought she owed him. Just like Tim.

This time Gaby struggled. She threshed against the iron restraint of his hold, half sobbing with humiliation and fear. She knew what happened next and she couldn't bear it. She *couldn't*.

Somehow he had managed to get her off balance. Her mind blanked in panic as she felt the room tilt and sway. Sven lifted her easily. He didn't take his lips from the pulse-point at the base of her throat where the thundering blood betrayed her fear.

'Don't,' she whispered.

Sven took no notice. He hardly seemed to hear her. He lowered her to the rug, quite gently, and then he was beside her kissing her not gently at all.

Gaby's eyes screwed tight shut. She was back in the nightmare. Last time there had been the sound of Jill's country and western music downstairs and the smell of brandy on Tim's breath. But that was all that was different. The rest — the man not hearing, her own half-guilty misery — was all horribly familiar.

He wrenched her T-shirt over her head, one possessive hand on her breast. Gaby whimpered.

She felt Sven pause, looking down at her. Instinctively, she turned her head away from that scrutiny. She heard him draw a long breath. Then suddenly, astonishingly, she was free.

For what seemed like hours Gaby lay there on the rug, not quite believing it. She could taste the salt of her own tears in the corner of her mouth. Then she began to realise that her bare skin was chilled. She clasped her arms round herself. Then she opened her eyes and looked around for her T-shirt.

Sven was sitting cross-legged at her feet, watching her gravely. Gaby flushed and avoided his eyes.

'I'm cold,' she muttered.

He tossed her an ornamental shawl from the back of one of the chairs. She would rather have had her T-shirt but she wasn't making an issue of it. She huddled it round her.

'Tell me.' It was quiet.

Gaby was surprised and her quick look told him so. At the very least she had expected recriminations; maybe accusations: You're cold. You don't give yourself. You're frigid.

She knew them all. Tim had accustomed her to them. Not just on that awful night but later, when she had said that she didn't want to do any more concerts with him.

She swallowed, clasping the silk shawl against her throat. Strands of loosened hair fell about her neck. She pushed them back with a hand that shook and saw Sven watch the movement, his eyes unreadable.

'Tell you what?' she muttered at last.

His mouth was wry. 'Why you went from being not afraid of anything or anyone to—this.'

Gaby bit her lip. She didn't know how to answer. He reached out and took one of her hands away from her throat. He did it very gently but she still went rigid as soon as he touched her.

'Look,' he said. He opened her clenched fingers, holding her hand between both of his. Gaby looked down at her palm. It was deeply scored with the marks of her nails. There could be no more eloquent evidence of abject panic.

'You were terrified, weren't you?'

She didn't answer. Sven sighed impatiently, pushing a hand through his hair. The sun struck light like flame from it. Gaby shuddered.

'Gabrielle——'

Gaby couldn't bear the gentle tone. 'Yes, I was scared,' she said quickly, hardly. 'What did you expect? We're alone in the middle of nowhere, as you've already pointed out. You're stronger than I am. A lot stronger. And you took great delight in telling me this morning that I wouldn't be able to get away from you.' She shook her hair out of her eyes. 'Put yourself in my place. Wouldn't you be scared?'

His eyes narrowed. 'You weren't afraid until just now.'

'Until you flung me on the floor,' Gaby corrected.

She saw him wince. It gave her a certain satisfaction though it didn't really make up for the fear. Even now, it was only just beginning to recede. She removed her hand from his clasp.

But he said, 'No, I don't think it's as simple as that.'

'You mean you don't want to believe it's as simple as that,' Gaby said bitterly. Tim could have been there at Sven's shoulder, reproachful and indignant. 'If you want a woman she has to want you back. And if she doesn't, then there's something wrong with her.'

There was a small silence. Then Sven said thoughtfully, 'Sounds to me as if you've known all the wrong men, Gabrielle Fouquet.'

Gaby jumped. 'What?'

'I don't think you're talking about me,' Sven told her. 'But you're talking about someone. Someone you know well. Maybe more than one.'

He was too perceptive. Gaby shuddered.

'It was you who jumped on me just now,' she pointed out in a high, breathless voice. 'Not some other party, whether I know them well or not.'

'True.' His eyes were alarmingly shrewd. 'But for quite a while back there you wanted me as much as I wanted you.'

She opened her mouth to deny it, met the grey eyes and shut it again.

'I'm not excusing myself. God knows, I shouldn't have let things get out of control like that,' Sven said levelly. 'But it wasn't just me. And you know it.'

Gaby stared at him. He was right. She thought of the

fire in her blood, the wild moments when she had stopped thinking altogether. Her hand went to her mouth in a gesture of shock.

Sven was implacable. 'Don't you?'

Gaby looked at him blankly.

'Gabrielle, if you hadn't remembered something nasty, you and I would be making love right now,' Sven Hedberg told her. He stood up and looked down at her consideringly.

'I'm going to find out what it is. We're going to deal with it. And then. . .' he gave her a slow smile '. . .we'll make love properly.

CHAPTER SIX

THE trouble was, Gaby thought as she prowled restlessly along the shore later under a threatening sky, she
wasn't quite sure whether he meant it. When she had
pulled out of the hold of his eyes and run for the open
air, she had been certain that he meant every word. As
she calmed down she was less certain.

There had been a battle going on, no question of
that. But she was beginning to suspect that the battle
between them was about power, not love, nor even
lust. And he had won, Gaby reflected bitterly. She was
the one who had run away.

She shivered when she remembered how thoroughly
he had won.

She kicked moodily at a clump of buttercups. What
on earth was she to make of the man? One day he was
warning her not to get romantic ideas about him, yet
the next he was saying with complete conviction that
they would make love. Properly. She even believed
him.

Gaby sat down at the water's edge. Where had it
come from, that lightning attraction? It had been there
right from that first day, that first kiss. One touch and
she had gone up in flames.

She pulled her plait over her shoulder, plucking
absently at the fronded ends. She thought Tim had
frozen all that sort of feeling out of her. She had seen
friends fall in love but after Tim she had thought that
that simply was not an option for her any more.

And yet. . . And yet. . .

She leaned forward, looking into the dark mirror that
was the lake. There were small ripples where the water
met the sedge. Behind the ripples she saw her own face,

the reflected expression deeply troubled. She put up a hand to touch her furrowed brow.

It was the same face as before — pointed chin and deep-set eyes, the usual fronds of hair escaping across her brow and cheek. So why did she suddenly look strange to herself? Gaby turned her hand over, the back against her warm cheek. Because Sven Hedberg had touched her?

It was a disturbing thought. Not least because he had not seemed in the least disturbed. Her reflection frowned quickly.

Oh, he had been interested enough. He had made no secret of it, after all. If Gaby had been willing no doubt they would be in bed together now.

She shivered a little at the thought. Just Sven Hedberg's imagined passion was enough to send little chills of alarm up and down her spine. What on earth would happen if he touched her seriously? She moistened her suddenly dry lips and said it to herself deliberately: *When* he touched her seriously.

What had their encounter meant to him? Barbro had called him wild and warned her off. Her father had talked of his reputation with women. Sven had virtually admitted it himself.

It would have been no big deal for him even if they had ended up making love as he clearly intended. So why did it throw Gaby into shaking confusion? After all, she was an expert on gentle evasion, if anyone was. Tim had taught her that if nothing else. So why could she not evade Sven Hedberg's negligent sexuality the way she evaded all the rest?

I must get out, she thought, in something like panic. I'm not sure what would happen if — when — he touches me again.

She crossed the bridge and walked for hours along the lake shore looking for the way. The path diverged frequently, taking off into clumps of pine trees. But it always came back to the water. There didn't seem to be any path big enough to lead to a settlement of some sort.

The sky got darker. In the end she was forced to turn back. For a moment she stood on the path with the trees meeting over her head and could see nothing. She was lost. But then, through the leaves, she caught the gleam of water.

She expelled a long breath of relief and dived towards it, leaving the shelter of the trees in her anxiety to get back to a landmark she recognised. If she had wanted evidence of how impossible it was to get away, here it was in stark relief.

It began to rain. Gaby started to run. She got back to the house soaked, as well as tired and defeated.

The first thing she saw when she went into the little dark hallway was Sven. His red hair was tousled and he had a pen behind his ear. He had also discarded his shirt. Gaby swallowed hard at the sight. Why was the smooth, tanned back so disturbing?

Sven seemed unaware of her turbulent feelings. Nor did he show any solicitude for her dripping state. If anything he looked smug.

'Failed to find an escape route?' he asked amiably.

Gaby was furious at his mockery — and the acuteness of his perception. She was also horribly conscious of their last encounter. She could still feel his hands on her skin, she thought with a shiver. Her eyes fell before his. That made her even angrier.

'Thank you for your concern,' she said sharply.

He looked amused. 'Surely a drop of rain doesn't upset a gypsy like you?'

Gaby looked down at her soaked T-shirt.

'More than a drop,' she said ruefully.

'So I see.' It was said gravely but there was a gleam in his eyes that made Gaby wish that she were less aware of him. And that he was more than half dressed.

She said with more than a touch of defiance, 'I'm going to have a bath.'

His look of amusement deepened. 'By all means.' His eyes went up and down her figure, dramatically revealed in her sodden clothing. Gaby's face flamed but all he said was a prosaic, 'Put the hot water in first. I'm not sure how much there is. The electricity has been less than reliable this afternoon.'

'I will,' she muttered. 'Thank you.' She fled past him up the creaking stairs.

He was right about the hot water. The bath was not much more than tepid. She bathed quickly and then wrapped herself in an elderly Arran sweater over her heaviest jeans. She was shivering by the time she had finished.

She took her hairbrush and went downstairs to the kitchen where the wood-burning stove was a haven of warmth. She took the bentwood chair as close to it as she could get. Carefully, Gaby began to brush her long, damp hair, fanning it into a silken mesh through which she could see the thunderous light beyond the window.

After a few minutes a small sound made her look up. Sven was standing in the doorway, an odd expression on his face.

She paused. The brush fell in her hand. A charged silence stretched between them.

Sven was still not wearing a shirt. Gaby could see from the way his chest lifted and fell that he was breathing as deeply as if he had been climbing a mountain. Something inside her craved to lay her hands against the golden ribs.

She looked away, putting the brush down carefully on the table.

He said in an odd voice, 'You were wet, weren't you? You need a drink. There should be something here that will warm you up.'

He investigated the contents of the painted dresser. Unseen, Gaby drew a steadying breath.

'Here it is.'

He withdrew a bottle of colourless liquid. It was unlabelled. Gaby put up her brows.

'Home-brewed?'

'Distilled. Almost certainly illegally.' He was laughing. 'Local rather than here in this house.' He uncorked the bottle and poured two small glasses. He pushed one across to her. 'Try it.'

Gaby picked it up and smelled it doubtfully. It had a faint odour of herbs. It seemed mild enough. Sven tossed his down in a single gulp. Cautiously, Gaby sipped her own — and gasped.

'What — is — that?' she said when she could speak. Her lips felt numb.

Sven chuckled. '*Brännvin*. Literally burning wine.'

'Well, that's a product description I won't quarrel with,' Gaby croaked. She put a hand to her throat. 'What *is* it?'

'The local version of schnapps. Specifically designed to keep the cold out.' His eyes glinted. 'Another?'

Gaby indicated her almost full glass.

'Drink up. It will make you feel better. Eventually,' he added, his mouth solemn.

Gaby looked at him in some dudgeon. She was learning to watch for that straight-faced teasing, she thought. In spite of that prim mouth, his eyes were dancing. He was clearly highly amused.

'I look forward to it,' she told him when she got her voice back. But she finished the glass. She felt that honour demanded it.

'You huddle up by the stove. I'll cook you a traditional Swedish midsummer dinner,' he said as one offering a concession. 'And we'll pretend there isn't a cloudburst going on out there.'

He poured her another glass of *brännvin*.

'Go on. Drink up and relax. Dry your hair.'

For an instant it seemed as if he laid his hand against the shining fall of her hair. But then he was reaching past her for a cast-iron pan. Gaby thought she must have imagined it.

He busied himself with the food. It seemed he was still interested in her afternoon's adventure.

'Go far?' he asked her.

Gaby looked eloquently out at the rain-lashed, deserted landscape.

'How can I tell? There don't seem to be any mile-stones in this wilderness. I didn't make it to any human habitation, if that's what you want to know.'

'I didn't think you would,' Sven said in a satisfied tone.

Gaby discovered that it was quite easy to resent him, notwithstanding the muscles and the tan.

'It must be nice to be infallible,' she said cordially.

The handsome mouth twitched. 'Oh, I make mistakes the same as everyone else.'

'You amaze me.'

He looked at her, his eyes unreadable. 'I'm not sure you weren't one of them.'

Gaby finished her *brännvin* and recklessly helped herself to a third. 'What do you mean?'

But he shook his head maddeningly. She leaned her elbows on the table, watching him scrub small potatoes. 'You know, you're not very logical. You really should make up your mind. Either you don't trust me an inch, in which case you ought to throw me out, not keep me imprisoned in your forest wilderness, or you think the therapy is worth a go. If you want to give it a try it doesn't make sense to keep sniping at me.' She bethought her of some of his accusations. 'Or making snide remarks about Michael,' she finished with slightly hazy indignation.

He looked at her curiously. For a moment he didn't speak. Then, 'You're very loyal. Does it ever occur to you he may not be worth it?'

'You sound like my mother,' said Gaby involuntarily.

Anne had very little respect for her ex-husband and his film-star clientele.

'She doesn't like you seeing a man so much older than you are?'

Gaby hesitated. Was it not time that she stopped this idea of his about her and Michael? 'It's not that,' she began, but he left her no time to continue.

'What does she do? Housewife and mother?'

Gaby smiled at the thought. 'She would get pretty steamed up if she could hear you. My mother is seriously committed to her career.'

'I've known some of them,' Sven said. He did not sound as if he had liked them. 'Give me a clue.'

Gaby hesitated. It seemed like surrendering a piece of herself to him. But that was stupid, she told herself. So she said quietly, 'Alternative therapies. My mother is Anne Fouquet. She is rather a pioneer in the field.'

Out of the corner of her eye she saw his eyebrows fly up in quick surprise.

'That Fouquet. Impressive. She worked on non-interventionist treatment for years with Johnson and Bailey.'

'Yes,' she agreed, surprised in her turn. 'Do you know their work?'

'I'm not quite as hidebound as you seem to think,' he said, amused. 'There's a long history of alternative medicine in Sweden. Not Hyssop's Hollywood non-sense, respectable alternative medicine.' A little laugh shook him. 'There's even a medicine called Swedish bitters that's used by homeopaths all over the world.'

Gaby looked at him in suspicion. Was he winding her up again? She could not see his eyes but his mouth was curling slightly at the corner.

'I've never heard of it.'

'Well, you should have. It was invented by a doctor in the middle of the last century.' He had put the potatoes into water and carried the saucepan to the stove. He slanted a look down at her, his expression innocent. 'It was so successful that it took a fall from his horse to kill him. He was supposed to be a hundred and four at the time,' he added.

He *was* winding her up. Gaby had to fight a strong desire to laugh. And an equally strong desire to let her head slip sideways until it rested against the muscled warmth of his thigh.

'Amazing,' she said huskily.

He was concentrating on regulating the heat under the potatoes. It seemed that her family relations still exercised his mind.

'So she doesn't like you working with Hyssop,' Sven mused. 'I'm not surprised. However way out Anne Fouquet may be, I've never heard that she was a charlatan.'

Gaby gave a sudden choke of laughter at the admission. Sven raised his brows.

'Who are you being rudest about? Michael or me?' she asked.

He gave her an odd smile. 'For a starry-eyed New Ager, you can be surprisingly shrewd,' he remarked. 'I was trying to suggest that Michael Hyssop may not be the best person in the world for a young girl like you to work with.'

Gaby shifted in her seat. The smile was making her distinctly uncomfortable. 'I am not a starry-eyed New Ager,' Gaby contradicted with precision. 'And I keep telling you, I'm not a child either.'

His eyes mocked her. 'Are you trying to tell me you don't believe in the harmony of earth, water and the human spirit? And the healing properties of all three? Is it needling you to say that you do?'

Gaby drew a long breath, meeting his gaze. There was mockery and something else in the brilliant eyes. This, she thought suddenly, was important.

'I believe there's more to the universe than science. And more to mankind than the intellect,' she said quietly.

The grey eyes searched her face, their expression enigmatic. He bent his head in acknowledgement. An odd little smile played about the handsome mouth.

At last he said in voice not much more than a whisper, 'You're saying we should listen to our instincts?'

Gaby couldn't tell if he was mocking her or not.

She said with dignity, 'If we want to be whole.'

'And if our instincts are in conflict?'

The soft question startled her. 'What?'

The mouth was twisted suddenly. 'Specifically your instincts and mine,' he explained. 'Which don't seem to be giving us the same messages.'

Gaby stared at him. Too late she realised where the conversation had led her. No, where *he* had led her. Deliberately and to his considerable amusement, as she could now see. Her eyes flashed at the sudden realisation.

'Not the same messages at all,' he mused.

He leaned towards her, and touched one long finger under her chin. Gaby arched away from it, her head rearing and her spine arching uncomfortably. She glared. His eyes danced suddenly, a wicked glint in their depths.

'Or are they?' He leaned even further forward, lowering over her. The crick in her neck became intolerable.

'You're going to fall off that chair, you know,' Sven said helpfully.

Before she knew what he was doing he had reached out and tipped her gently on to the rug in front of the stove. With a small exclamation of fury Gaby collapsed.

Sven came down beside her in one smooth movement. He bent over her. It infuriated Gaby to see that he was still laughing.

'A small experiment,' he said softly. 'Lie back and think of cosmic harmony.'

Gaby resisted as hard as she could. But with one

elbow awkwardly trapped under her and her other wrist
bent back at an excruciating angle against the hard wall
of his naked chest she was next to helpless. She turned
her head away from those dancing eyes.

'You're not being fair,' she complained on a ragged
breath.

His hand swept explicitly down the length of heavy
denim to her bare ankle. In spite of herself, Gaby felt
her heart contract in a little shudder of longing. She
knew he felt it too. It filled her with shame.

'I'm not a fair man.' Sven sounded amused. He
slipped a hand under her thick sweater. Her flesh had
lost its chill in the last half-hour and now his fingers
moved against the soft, warm skin of her waist. Gaby
screwed her eyes tight shut. 'On the other hand, I am
honest,' he murmured. 'Unlike you, I think.'

Gaby tried hard to close her mind to the waves of
sensation produced by that cynical hand. This is all
about power, she reminded herself. He wants to prove
that he can subjugate me completely. He wants to
punish me for associating with Michael. He wants. . .

Her eyes flew open as his fingers travelled. She
managed not to react otherwise to the silken touch
against the underside of her breast — just. His eyes were
very close. She met them.

'Honest?' It was little more than a ragged breath.

A smile curved his mouth. Not a kind smile.

'I admit what I want. You——' his hand caressed her
breast slowly so that Gaby had to suppress a gasp
'—don't.'

She folded her lips together and fought for control.
'At least I don't take my anger out on people who are
only trying to help me,' she said on a gasp.

The questing hand stilled. His eyebrows twitched
together. The humour left his face as if it had been
wiped clean.

'Anger?' he said at last in a soft, icy voice that made
Gaby shiver inside.

She struggled up on one elbow. 'Isn't that what this is about? I touched a nerve of some sort this morning. You haven't forgiven me. You're not pretending that you've fallen in love with me, I notice.'

He stared down at her. Then, quite suddenly, he lifted himself away. Gaby repressed a sigh of relief.

'There are other options, you know,' Sven told her drily. 'It doesn't have to be anger or love. There are a lot of feelings in between.'

He sat up, looking down at her. Unobtrusively, Gaby shifted sideways, setting a small but important space between them. His mouth quirked.

'Don't like honest lust, Gabrielle?'

It was a challenge.

'I don't like people playing power games with me,' she told him quietly.

He looked honestly surprised. 'And that's what you feel when I touch you? Power games?'

And a wholly unwelcome sensation of being borne along on a tidal wave. But she wasn't going to tell him that.

'Power games,' Gaby said firmly.

He shook his head in mock-bewilderment. 'I must do something about my technique. No one's ever said that to me before.'

'Never mind technique, try doing something about your feelings,' Gaby snapped. It was pure reflex and she regretted it the moment she said it. 'I imagine your usual line of ladies are too polite to complain,' she added hastily.

But his eyes had narrowed at her too revealing retort.

'You'd be happier if I pretended to be in love with you?'

Gaby winced at the thought. Tim had said he was in love with her. All that had meant was that he felt he didn't have to consider her feelings any more.

Sven said softly, 'I see it wouldn't. Interesting.' He looked down at her. 'What have you got against love?'

'Nothing. I —'

'At your age I would have thought you were waiting breathlessly for it to arrive.'

Gaby eyed him with disfavour. 'You really don't have much of an opinion of me at all, do you? How silly do you think I am?'

'Waiting for love isn't silly at twenty-four,' he said, surprising her. 'One learns, of course, as one gets older. But you are —'

'Too stupid to learn?' Gaby flashed.

'No.' He surveyed her for a moment and then said slowly, 'No, I wouldn't have said stupid. But you're young. Too young to be disillusioned. And you've rather pinned your colours to the mast in the heart versus head debate, haven't you?'

She looked at him in frustration. He was too clever.

'In principle,' said Gaby with dignity.

'But not in practice? Interesting,' he said again.

She made a dismissive gesture.

'So you're not too young to be disillusioned,' Sven mused. 'What happened? Did you turn up on Hyssop's doorstep unannounced and find him with someone else?'

Gaby gave a choke of astonished laughter which she did not suppress quickly enough. Sven's eyes narrowed to slits.

'Even more interesting.'

Gaby met his eyes defiantly. 'I don't see why. My private feelings have nothing to do with you.'

He ignored that. 'So it wasn't Hyssop. What was it, Gabrielle? Unrequited love? Or some boy of your own age who grew tired of being teased?'

Gaby froze. He knows, she thought numbly. He can't. But he does. He knows about Tim. Tim had said it was her fault. That she was a tease. He had said if she hadn't led him on. . .

'Or both?' Sven suggested gently.

Gaby swallowed, her throat suddenly dry. She didn't answer. She couldn't. He looked at her speculatively.

'I don't know how you found out,' she said in scratchy tones, 'but it isn't what you think.'

'And what do I think?' he challenged her softly.

Gaby had no doubt about that. 'That I was playing games. But I wasn't. I don't. I'm not like you.' She was upset and barely coherent. 'I didn't know. Didn't realise. . .'

'Didn't realise what?'

Gaby felt the old sadness wash over her. Sadness and a bewildered anger. What could she say? That after so many sandwich lunches on the steps of Prince Albert's statue, after this many concerts and that many shared rehearsals, she didn't have a choice any more about whether she went to bed with Tim? It was a desolate thought.

No, she couldn't say that to Sven Hedberg. If she couldn't say it to friends or to her parents, she certainly couldn't say it to this ice-hearted stranger.

She said carefully, 'He was a colleague. I didn't know he felt strongly about me.' That much at least was true.

'You didn't care about him?'

Gaby bit her lip. 'He was a friend,' she said in a low voice.

That was one of the worse things, losing a friend. Especially one who was part of the cheerful shared household.

'What happened?' he said again. His voice was surprisingly gentle.

Gaby drew a shaky breath. Then she thought suddenly, Why not? Go on, tell him. He won't care. And it might do you good to talk. You never have. He doesn't know Tim. He won't blame him and if he does it won't matter. Anyway, you don't care what he thinks.

She bent her head and looked at the rug with minute attention.

'It was after a concert. We used to play together,' she

said in a low voice. 'Tim's a violinist. It was a good performance. We—I suppose we were both a bit high with it.'

They had been excited as children, running into the small bistro afterwards hand in hand, to the vociferous admiration of friends. Other people in the restaurant had looked indulgent at the spontaneous applause that had greeted them. Some had been envious, some wistful; but they had all thought that Tim and Gaby were on top of the world. Which made it all the worse that two hours later. . .

She ran her tongue over her dry lips.

'I didn't realise,' she said again. 'I liked him. We worked well together. But he'd never said anything——'

'And that night he decided you were going to crown your success?' Sven suggested cynically.

Gaby shook her head. 'I don't think he decided anything. I—hope he didn't. No, I'm sure he didn't. He's not a schemer. He wouldn't plot. He just thought—he must have thought—that we already had a love-affair in the making.' Her voice rasped. She had thought about this over and over again until her head spun and she still couldn't make sense of it.

'And you didn't?'

'I—— No,' she said in a subdued tone. 'No, I didn't think of him like that.'

'You told him so?'

That was a question. Had she? Had she said in so many words, Tim, I don't want to go to bed with you? Hadn't she rather dodged and evaded and deflected until it was too late to do anything but endure?

She bent her head. 'I—I'm not sure.'

'Well, that's honest,' he said coolly.

Gaby's head came up, startled. But she couldn't summon the anger that she knew the negligent comment deserved.

She said again wretchedly, 'I didn't know he thought

of me like that. I'd never seen any sign of it. He said
I'd been leading him on. You're right about that. But I
never realised. He never *said*.'

'There are other forms of communication,' Sven
commented.

Gaby sighed. 'I know. I must have been stupid. I just
didn't notice. Until that night, it never occurred to me
that Tim wanted me for anything more than a friend.'

Sven went suddenly still. 'Until that night?' he
echoed softly.

She coloured. 'After the concert.'

'I realise that. What happened after the concert?'

'Tim took me home. I — we — lived in a shared house
with three others. Tim's room was on the first floor. I
had the attic. He — he came up to the attic.'

'Had he never been there before?'

'Never at midnight,' said Gaby with a little remembered shiver. 'He'd come up to practise because that's
where I had the piano. But otherwise we'd talk in the
kitchen. Most of the house social life went on in the
kitchen.'

Sven said slowly, 'Are you telling me you didn't
date?'

'Not — not in the way you mean. We went to concerts
together sometimes because we were both involved
with music. But we never went anywhere else on our
own. There were always other people around. He never
met my family. I never met his. We went to the same
parties because we knew a lot of the same people. But
we didn't go as a pair. We never went away together.'

The grey eyes were inscrutable. 'Then how did you
lead him on?'

Gaby shook her head slowly. 'I don't know. I've
thought about it and thought about it. We'd never even
kissed except. . .'

'Except?'

'Well, socially. When we met sometimes, that sort of
thing. And that night, after our concert, I was so happy

I gave him a big hug. I suppose he thought it meant more than it did.' All her confusion and guilty misery was in her voice.

Sven looked at her searchingly. 'He doesn't seem to have had a lot of grounds. What did he do to you, Gabrielle?'

His voice was quite gentle but Gaby had the impression of a strong emotion at work. She thought she detected anger again and winced. He made a sharp movement, quickly stilled.

Taking her courage in her hands, Gaby said rapidly, 'He wanted to make love and when I wouldn't he made me do it anyway.'

She had said it. At last it was out in plain words. For the first time she had told the truth about that terrible night. Oddly it felt as if she was admitting it to herself as well as to Sven. Gaby realised that she felt as if an iron weight had fallen off her shoulders.

The silence was absolute. She couldn't look at Sven. She felt very cold again. She huddled her arms round and propped her back up against the stove.

He said in a neutral voice, 'How long ago was this — misunderstanding?'

She swallowed. 'Three years.'

'What have other people said about it?'

'I — haven't told anyone. I couldn't. I sort of felt — guilty.'

'You have not told anyone else?' Sven's voice was very soft.

She shook her head. Her drying hair was a cloud around her, hiding her expression. 'Not till now.'

'Not Hyssop?'

'No.'

'And you've carried it around as if it happened yesterday,' he diagnosed.

Gaby bit her lip. 'It's not as bad as that. I admit I'm — wary.'

He touched a fingertip to her lower lip and watched her jerk away. 'Wary?'

Her lashes fell. 'You must think I'm the most awful fool.'

His eyes came back to meet her own. 'Fool? No. Too trusting maybe. But you were young. You are still too young to —— ' He broke off, sounding bitter suddenly. His eyes shifted. He stood up swiftly and looked down at her.

'Food,' he said with a brisk change of tone which made Gaby blink. 'You're light-headed and so am I. I'll get some clothes on and you can set the table in the dining-room.'

He did not extend a hand down to help her to her feet, she noticed. Nor did his eyes quite meet her as she stood up.

But at the door he paused and said abruptly, 'It's a long time since I knew anyone who was too trusting. I'm not sure those are rules I know.'

CHAPTER SEVEN

WHEN Sven came downstairs again he was wearing a creamy linen shirt and dark trousers. Watching from the door of the dining-room, Gaby watched him pushing up the shirt-sleeves impatiently, as if he had a distasteful task to perform. She came out of the shadows.

'Table set,' she said cheerfully.

The main light in the hall flickered. He narrowed his eyes at it.

'The storm is probably getting closer. We'd better have candles. They're in the kitchen dresser.'

Gaby had already seen a branch of glass candlesticks in the dining-room, curlicued and decorated in the shape of reeds and leaping mermaids. It had struck her as ornate, in contrast with the rest of this plain house, and when they were seated she said so.

Sven was lighting the candles with a lighter he had produced from his pocket. He stopped briefly at her comment and surveyed the candlestick.

'I suppose you're right.' He sounded surprised. 'My mother brought it back from one of her travels. It's Venetian.'

He lit the last candle and sat down. Outside the sky was darkening ominously. The light from the candles was a relief, making the simple room seem suddenly warmer and friendlier as well as less full of shadows.

'She travelled a lot?' asked Gaby, watching him set a painted earthenware dish of some small fish between them.

'As much as she could manage.' Sven sounded quite indifferent.

Gaby remembered that Barbro had said his father hated his mother's absence.

'Was she a doctor too?'

He shook his head. The candlelight drew flickers of silver and true crimson from his hair. He looked impossibly handsome, with the austere profile thrown into Renaissance relief. Gaby's unreliable heart gave a lurch.

'No. She was rich enough not to be anything. She dabbled in a lot of things. She was very easily bored.' There was no condemnation in his tone.

'Is that why she travelled?'

'Oh, no. She always wanted to see new things. She was a natural traveller. And——' he smiled '—well, to be honest she was a natural consumer as well. We Swedes are very puritanical about money. For years we had a government which taxed very heavily. Everyone was supposed to have the same amount of money to live on, you see. If you earned any more, it had to go back to the State to be used for the good of everybody. Kristin wasn't that puritanical. She kept most of her personal fortune outside the country and stayed away enough to make sure that she did not have Swedish residence.'

'Oh,' said Gaby thoughtfully. So his mother had gone travelling because she had wanted to avoid Swedish taxation. It had not been the children's fault after all. Well, Barbro had said it wasn't. She said carefully, 'That must have been hard on the rest of you.'

He sent her a shrewd look. 'Barbro managed to pack a lot in, didn't she?' he said drily. 'I don't think it made much difference to us as children. We were always well cared for. It was hardest on my father. He adored her. But he didn't approve of her. That can be tough.' He pushed a plate towards her. 'Help yourself.'

Gaby was reluctant to leave the subject.

'Did you approve of her?'

He shrugged. 'I don't make those sort of judgements.'

'But you must know whether you. . .'

He gave a little exasperated sigh and leaned forward to ladle potatoes on to her plate.

'Eat. Stop digging up old stories that don't matter any more.'

Gaby watched him under her lashes. He had spoken with real feeling for a second when he had said it was tough to adore someone you disapprove of.

'Don't they?'

'This,' he said deliberately, 'is standard midsummer fare in Sweden. We put dill on the potatoes, you will see. We use a lot of dill. You'll find it growing outside, virtually wild. We also use it in *gravad lax*, if you've ever had that. It is pieces of salmon marinaded in dill and vinegar and then packed up and pressed under a heavy weight. In the old days they used to bury it under a stone.'

'You're avoiding the subject,' Gaby said.

He smiled and helped her to the little fish.

'*Sill*,' he said in the same vein of instruction. 'Small herring. They're marinaded raw. These were done by Barbro but you can buy them in the shops already prepared. You eat them with sour cream —— ' he put a glass dish in front of her containing a pale swirl ' — with chives chopped up in it. I,' he added, 'chopped the chives. They're also growing outside. Quite a lot are in flower. Help yourself. Eat.'

'And stop asking difficult questions?' Gaby said wryly.

But she did as she was bid. She tasted the food. It was cool and aromatic, not as salty as she had expected.

'Delicious,' she said.

Sven watched her. He had not touched his own food.

'You know, you're a contradiction,' he said abruptly. 'Sharp as a needle at one moment, then — blank. Innocent, I suppose.' He began to eat. 'So what about you?

Do you approve of Michael Hyssop? Is there a conflict between that and what you feel for him? If you work with Anne Fouquet you will know that there are standards of professional behaviour.' His voice was hard suddenly. 'That ethical practitioners don't pass on their patients' affairs to the papers.'

Gaby looked down at her plate. 'That's different,' she began uncomfortably.

'No, it isn't. It's exactly the same.' Sven leaned forward suddenly, the red hair brilliant in the candle-flame. 'Don't you have any doubts about him at all? A man like that?'

'You're not fair to him,' she said, her voice unhappy. 'The piece about you was a mistake. . .'

He dismissed that with a wave of his fork. 'Never mind me. What about *you*? You're young. Talented. It's obvious you could do better for yourself than dressing up like a gypsy and playing 1940's hits if you wanted to. Why don't you? So you can follow Hyssop round the world? Can't you see the waste of it?'

Gaby stared into his eyes. The candle-flames were reflected in them in little points of flickering sharpness. They felt like lasers. Sven looked furious suddenly, as if he could barely contain his anger.

She drew back in her chair, moving deliberately out of the light cast by the candles.

He swore softly. 'For Heaven's sake, Gabrielle. Face it. You could have everything if you wanted. If you gave up Hyssop and just looked at what is there. I repeat, you're young, talented—and beautiful.'

She snorted. Sven went very still.,

'Hasn't he even made you realise how beautiful you are?' he said in a still voice. His chair made a scraping noise in the silence, which made her jump. He stood up and came round the table to her. Gaby's protest froze in her throat under the mesmerising look in his eyes.

'You sit there with your hair all around you like a naiad, like something out of a man's dreams——'

Of her own volition she seemed to be coming to her feet. He reached out almost reverently and wove one hand into the waving tresses, holding it up to the light.

'You're too damned innocent,' he whispered. 'You say you're wary but in fact you trust too much. You should not trust me, Gabrielle. You should not trust me at all.'

Her head was falling back, her eyes closing. She felt his breath against the sensitive skin of her eyelids. Then his lips, very gently. Then she was free.

Bewildered, Gaby opened her eyes. Sven's face in the dramatic shadows was harsh. He put his thumb against her mouth before she could ask what was the matter. It was a clear rejection.

'I'd be no better than Hyssop if I took advantage of that,' he said bitterly. 'Go to bed, Gabrielle. There's going to be a storm.' She stared at him. 'Go to bed,' he said again fiercely.

She flinched as if he had hit her. She fled to the door. The harsh voice followed her.

'And if you're scared of the lightning, don't come to me in the night,' he told her.

Gaby barely noticed the lightning, though it lit the sky like day at times. She huddled in her bed tormented by thoughts which made the thunder overhead seem tame.

She turned and turned, desperately trying to forget how it had felt to be in his arms. In the first shock of being in his embrace, she had turned to him in love. Bitterly she castigated herself for that. What was between them was not love or anything like it. On her part it was a sort of fascinated curiosity, she told herself. It was fuelled by that dangerous excitement, of course. Sexual excitement, she said to herself deliberately. Not love.

And on Sven's part? Well, she didn't know because he wasn't telling. But she could guess.

He wanted her, had probably wanted her from the

first. But he had his rules. His women had to stay
uninvolved. And he had realised there was a danger
that Gaby would not manage to stay uninvolved. That
was a cruel blow to her pride. Because of course it was
true.

He wants to seduce me, she told herself, as the storm
raged outside. The only thing that's stopping him is that
he doesn't want to pay the price. He has no doubt at all
that he could have me if he wanted me.

It was a frightening thought for a girl who had prided
herself on being armoured.

He was too experienced, thought Gaby. Too clever.
No one else in three years had detected what Tim had
done to her. But it had taken Sven Hedberg less than
three days to see that she had been hurt — and to make
her tell him about it in graphic detail. He had made her
tell him things, in fact, that she had almost pushed out
of her memory because they were so painful.

Oh, he was clever all right. And Barbro was right —
he was dangerous. She would have to be very careful.

It soon became evident the next day, and the days
that followed, that she was not the only one being
careful.

Sven worked hard, merely emerging for meals and
for the music therapy sessions. He was interested in
Anne's progress chart and helped Gaby complete it at
the end of each session. There were a few idle questions
about her childhood and he asked about her work with
Anne. He never brought up Michael's name at all.

While for her part Gaby stayed rigidly with the
programme that Anne had outlined. She lived from day
to day and waited for the interval of incarceration to
end. She and Sven were carefully polite to each other.
Just occasionally they skirted what she was sure they
both felt would be disaster. One such occasion was
when she lost her temper at the end of an unproductive
therapy hour.

'This is hopeless. There are too many no-go areas.'

'No-go areas?'

'You don't talk about your feelings, I don't talk about mine,' Gaby pointed out drily.

He contemplated his circling wrist. 'I'm perfectly willing to talk about my feelings.' He sounded amused.

Gaby fought down a blush. After two weeks of his exclusive company, she had come to know Sven Hedberg rather well. She had learned to recognise when he was teasing her. So she raised her eyebrows and said sweetly, 'About anything serious?'

His mouth quirked. 'Serious for whom?' he asked huskily.

Although she knew now when he was winding her up, Gaby could not prevent the faint colour rising. If only that voice didn't send little rivulets of pleasure running down her spine. If only, she thought ruefully, he didn't know that it did just that.

But Sven Hedberg was a very experienced man and he knew to a microsecond the kind of tremors he could induce with no more than a few husky words and a slanting smile. And even though he did not want to risk serious involvement, he was not above teasing her.

He was not only dangerous, thought Gaby, meeting the faint challenge in his eyes with indignation, he had absolutely no scruples whatsoever.

She said with dignity, 'By serious I mean something with consequences. Something you won't forget you ever felt within a few weeks of it coming to an end.'

There was a little silence. Then he nodded, as if conceding a point in chess.

'Serious indeed,' he said lightly. But his expression was inscrutable. Gaby suddenly realised where the conversation was leading.

'Not that it's any business of mine,' she said hastily.

He put his head on one side. His eyes glinted with amusement. 'I wouldn't say that.'

She said in sudden exasperation, 'What do you want of me, Sven?'

The steady eyes flickered briefly.

'A very good question.'

She stamped her foot then. 'It amuses you to wind me up,' she said bitterly. 'Is that why you're keeping me here? So you can taunt me whenever you get bored?'

Sven laughed out loud at that. 'What a dramatic girl you are. You know why I'm keeping you here.'

Gaby looked at him narrowly. 'Do I?'

His face was very still. 'Think about it,' he advised softly.

Gaby gave a little shiver. The tone did things to her imagination which she didn't want to acknowledge. Not to herself; certainly not to him. She pulled herself together.

'It's a contest, isn't it?' she said bitterly. 'I'm supposed to help you find a cure for your hand tremor in spite of the fact that you have no respect for Michael and no trust in his treatments. And I'm the scapegoat if it all goes wrong.' she surveyed him unflatteringly. 'It's like something out of a fairy-tale.'

He wasn't noticeably cast down by her scorn. 'Oh, it is,' he agreed cordially.

Gaby glared. 'Don't you have any scruples at all?'

He seemed to consider that. 'About as many as you,' he decided.

'I've never kept anyone locked up in the middle of the forest,' Gaby flashed.

Sven sighed. 'Suffering from chocolate bar deprivation? All right. I'll take you out into the wide world.' He sent her a narrow-eyed look. 'As long as I can rely on your word not to run away.'

'I don't run away,' Gaby said with dignity.

'No,' he said slowly, an arrested expression on his face. 'No, you don't do you?'

She was surprised, though she didn't show it in case he changed his mind.

'Whereabouts in the wide world?' she said suspiciously. 'Somewhere with pavements and street-lights?'

'Not Stockholm,' he said with a chuckle. 'But we can go to town. It's the midsummer celebrations tomorrow. I usually go. And you ought to see something of Swedish culture while you're here.'

'Midsummer celebrations?' Gaby stared at him.

'The longest day. It's important for those of us who live with limited daylight most of the year,' Sven reminded her drily. 'The local amateur musicians turn out. There are stalls selling local carvings. There's a barbecue in the street. And you can dance all night if you like.'

'You're taking me *dancing*?' Gaby said in disbelief.

A shadow of annoyance passed across the handsome face.

'How old do you think I am, Gabrielle? I do dance.'

He was as good as his word.

'Come along,' he said to her as soon as they got out of the Land Rover the next evening. 'Tour of the town.' He took her hand proprietorially. 'Don't get lost.'

The tour of the town took ten minutes. Apart from one wide main street, there were three paths that wound down to the lakeside and another, wider street that climbed the gentle slope of the hillside. There were thirty houses or so, Gaby guessed. But the main street was full.

'Where do they all come from?' she asked.

Sven laughed. 'The woods. Up and down the lake. Stockholm. Minnesota.'

'What?' said Gaby, taken aback.

'This is the binge of the year,' Sven explained. 'Families come from miles away. Tourists too. Didn't you see the boats?'

'Yes, I suppose I did,' Gaby admitted.

There were all sorts of them, drawn up by the wooden dock. She was particularly taken with some of the larger ones, brightly coloured specimens with enormous oars that looked as if they could sail to America if they put their mind to it. She said so.

'Church boats,' Sven said briefly. 'A feature of a widely spread population.' His mouth curled in amusement. 'Source of a fair amount of not very Christian rivalry between some of the villages as well. The decoration is a local skill.'

'It's wild,' Gaby said with approval.

'It's actually rigidly conventional.' He slanted a look down at her. 'Just different conventions from the ones you're used to.'

Gaby swallowed. There was a message there that had nothing to do with the brilliant boats, she thought. She removed her hand from his.

'And what are the conventions for tonight? The binge of the year, as you call it.'

He calmly repossessed her hand. Gaby tried to resist but he seemed not to notice. And he was too strong for her to extract her hand without making a real production of it, she thought. She bit her lip.

'People walk round, see friends, look at the stalls. Then we go down to the dock. There will be a fiddlers' competition, I expect. There usually is. Then the barbecue. Some display dancing—local groups, children sometimes. The big celebration takes place round midnight. Then we all join in.'

The circulation in her hand was seriously threatened, Gaby thought. She eased her fingers in his. Sven's grip relaxed slightly. He still said nothing. Nor did he let her go.

Gaby cleared her throat. 'Display dancing? It's not just bopping in the streets, then?'

Sven looked amused. 'Don't let Barbro hear you say that, please. She takes it very seriously. The group meets every week in the winter. And they seem to get obsessed just before midsummer. It's very skilful. Wait till you see it.'

He was the perfect companion, Gaby found slightly

to her surprise—informed, entertaining and astonishingly spontaneous in his own enjoyment. And astonishingly sociable. He introduced her to a dozen people who appeared delighted to see him. And they were invited to join a cheerful crowd as everyone had converged on the tiny landing-stage.

Many of them were in national costume, Gaby saw. The women wore plain gathered skirts in what she assumed were natural dyes: sky-blue, rust, black. Their blouses were exquisitely crisp white cotton. The whole ensemble was turned into a rainbow by the addition of brilliant woven pinafores and scarves, draped over their shoulders and knotted in front. The men were no less colourful though they did not go for the rainbow look, Gaby saw. Mostly they wore dark breeches and stockings with full-sleeved shirts, the colour coming from the bright sleeveless waistcoat that topped it off.

'Have you got one of those?' she murmured to Sven, nodding at a man in a scarlet waistcoat heavily encrusted with a cable of black embroidery.

He chuckled. 'You're determined to know all my secrets, aren't you, Gabrielle? Well, there are some things a man has to keep back. For his self-respect.'

'I bet you have.'

But he shook his head, laughing, and would not tell her.

The air was full of smoke from the barbecue and the distant sound of virtuoso fiddle practice.

Sven found her an upturned barrel to sit on and supplied her with a plate of grilled meat and a glass of something cloudy and pungent. It was not the *brännvin*, Gaby found, sipping cautiously, but something altogether less risky. He went back to fetch his own food, threading his way unfalteringly through the crowd with the ease of long practice. Gaby watched him with a smile she was quite unaware of.

'Miss Hyssop,' said a voice in her ear.

Gaby jumped, nearly overturning her plate. She turned.

'I'm sorry?'

A man strolled round the corner of the piled barrels. He was tall and alone. He was dressed in dark trousers and a casual shirt that somehow looked expensive. Among the friendly crowd he looked out of place in a way that Sven Hedberg did not.

'Anders Storstrom,' he reminded her ruefully.

'Oh.' The man Sven despised. She bent her head in acknowledgement of his greeting. 'Hello,' she said awkwardly. 'Are you here for the midsummer celebrations?'

His smile did not reach his eyes, she saw. 'Hardly. My readers don't go much for folklore.'

'So what do they go for?' asked Gaby. She did not like the way he was looking at her and wished he would go away.

'Oh, people,' he said vaguely. There was an amusement in his voice which, she thought, didn't sound kind. 'Human interest is what sells papers, after all.'

'You're honest, at least,' said an icy voice.

Anders Storstrom swung neatly round. His expression conveyed surprise but Gaby had the distinct impression that he was not surprised at all. And that he was pleased.

Her vague suspicion of him grew.

'Doctor!' he exclaimed. 'Twice in a month. What a coincidence.'

'Is it?' Sven asked drily. He put down the plate he was carrying very carefully. It was almost as if he was bracing himself for a fist fight, Gaby thought, watching the two men. She looked from one to the other and felt troubled.

'What are you suggesting, Doctor? That I'm here to check up on you? And your charming companion, of course.' He shook his head sadly. 'You wrong me. I'm the proprietor of a respectable newspaper chain. I don't chase scandal stories.'

'Somebody else does the leg work these days?' Sven enquired softly.

A faint hint of annoyance marred the dazzling smile. But Storstrom did his best to stay charming.

'So you're admitting that there is a story?'

Sven's eyes locked with the other man's. Gaby thought she had never seen such icy fury in his face before.

'I hardly see that my private activities are of interest to anyone but myself and my friends.'

'Come along, Doctor.' Storstrom sounded almost brisk. 'There's always a story where a famous man is concerned.'

Very slowly Sven shook his head. 'No,' he said quite gently.

Gaby tensed at the tone. She had never heard Sven speak in that voice before. As if he would have no mercy on anyone who crossed him. Storstrom seemed not to notice the menace, though.

'Have you known that lady long? Where did you meet? Taken her home to meet the family? Does Serena Weissman know you've replaced her?'

Sven said nothing. Looking at the glacial profile, Gaby felt her heart turn over.

'Look. . .' she began.

Storstrom turned to her. 'How does it feel to catch yourself Sweden's most eligible bachelor? Elusive eligible bachelor,' he amended with a laugh.

Gaby sent a look at Sven. All his attention was fixed on the man in front of him.

'You've made enough mischief in my family, Storstrom. Content yourself with that.'

The other raised his eyebrows. The smile disappeared. 'Are you accusing me of printing lies? I never saw a writ for libel,' he said softly.

'I don't accuse you of printing lies,' Sven said carefully. He looked at his opponent measuringly. 'I think you're a rat, Storstrom, not an idiot. I accuse you of making people's private troubles the raw material of your profit. Of not caring whom you hurt or what it does to them as long as you make money.'

Storstrom shrugged. 'That's business, my friend.' His eyes had sharpened. 'And whose private troubles are we talking about here? Your lovely companion's? Hasn't she realised you dump them when the party's over?'

Sven said very quietly, 'I advise you to leave.'

Storstrom laughed.

Gaby didn't see Sven move. But all of a sudden Strostrom was staggering backwards, his hand flung up, an expression of almost comical amazement on his face.

'Careful,' Sven said. 'The dock's slippery.'

He took hold of Storstrom's arm. The man tried to shake him off. They swayed for a few seconds, then, before Gaby's disbelieving eyes, Anders Storstrom fell backwards into the water. One moment he was strug-gling for balance, glaring at the man who held him by the shoulder, the next he was flying spread-eagled through the air.

Gaby darted forward. Sven glanced down as if her presence startled him. His eyes were blazing.

The incident did not go unnoticed. There wasn't general alarm and despondency, Gaby saw. In fact the willing hands that hauled Storstrom out belonged to people who obviously thought it was a tremendous joke. They also didn't seem to be at all surprised.

Storstrom's expression was ugly. Gaby moved instinctively closer to Sven. He put an arm round her, his hand twining a stray chestnut curl round her ear.

'Don't worry,' he said coolly. 'People always fall in the water at midsummer. More than one person will follow him before the evening's out.'

Gaby swallowed. 'But he didn't exactly fall, did he? You pushed him.'

Sven gave a soft laugh. He shrugged 'He'd have difficulty proving it.'

She shook her head. This was a responsible, respected man, she reminded herself.

'*Why?*'

His mouth slanted. All of a sudden his expression was hard.

'Lots of reasons. He had it coming. Especially from me. Maybe one day I'll tell you.'

Gaby digested that.

'So it wasn't what he said about — whatever her name was — Selina someone?'

'Serena,' Sven supplied after a pause. 'Serena Weissman.'

Gaby looked away. 'Is she your girlfriend?'

Sven made an impatient noise. 'We had an arrangement,' he said uninformatively.

'Oh.'

Gaby thought it over. Of course. He would have an arrangement with someone. Sven Hedberg was an attractive man and frighteningly adult. He wouldn't live without female companionship. He wouldn't need to. It would be on his own terms, of course.

It doesn't matter to me what he does, Gaby thought fiercely. I don't care how many Serena Weissmans there are in his life. I'll never see him again once this month is up.

But that was where her whirling thoughts stopped dead. She tried hard to assure herself that she didn't want to see him again.

And yet she, who had thought she couldn't let any man touch her again after Tim, had melted in his arms like warm toffee. It was only chemistry, she told herself a little desperately. But even if it was only a chemical reaction, could she really bear to say goodbye to him forever? Never explore what might happen if the reaction was allowed to continue to explosion point?

Gaby's mouth dried at the thought. 'Oh, lord,' she said under her breath.

She was conscious of a hollow feeling. She identified it without too much trouble. It was what she felt like before a concert. It was half-excitement, half-trepidation and wholly terrifying. She also had a nasty feeling that she knew exactly why she was feeling this way about the man beside her who was looking at her in an irritated fashion.

'Serena and I were perfectly in accord about our relationship,' he said with deliberation. 'It isn't anybody's business but ours.'

Gaby swallowed. 'Of course not,' she murmured.

'So will you please stop looking at me as if I eat a virgin every full moon?' Sven said, exasperated.

Gaby jumped and pulled herself together. She didn't want him detecting the direction of her thoughts.

'I didn't know I was. I'm sorry.'

'You have a very transparent face,' Sven told her thoughtfully. He touched the pale skin below her cheekbones and watched her reaction. Gaby felt her colour rise. 'It isn't always comfortable to know so clearly what you're thinking,' he said wryly.

Gaby repressed a shiver. 'I wish you didn't,' she said involuntarily.

His eyebrows twitched together. She had the feeling that he was going to say something important. For a moment she held her breath.

But then the music from the distant fiddlers suddenly grew loud. A group of men in leather waistcoats with violins at their chins appeared marching up the road to the harbour. Sven gave a little exclamation of frustration. But Gaby could only feel reprieved.

'Music,' she said unnecessarily.

The crowd had been milling about in a formless way. The children had been running up and down the dock, jumping on piles of wood and leaping on to capstans. The adults had been eating or drinking in groups. Now, at some unobtrusive sign from whoever was organising the celebration, the prettily costumed younger girls were moving about the lakeside, gathering up plates and plastic cups while everyone else formed a circle.

The fiddlers paraded into the middle of it, playing. The circle split to let them in and closed again at once. Gaby found Sven urging her forward, so that she stood in front of him with no one between herself and the musicians. She could feel the warmth of him at her back like a rock. He kept his hands on her shoulders. She could feel their warmth too, right through her.

It wasn't easy to concentrate on the music.

When the dancing started it was easier to pretend absorption. There were patterns to follow in the movements and some of the figures were very skilled. Gaby caught sight of Barbro, her face set in lines of concentration. Barbro did not see them. She was clearly not seeing anyone but her companions in the dance.

Sven bent. Gaby tensed as she felt the brush of his mouth against her ear. But all he said was, 'They win prizes, you know.'

Gaby looked at the serious faces and whirling, stamping figures. She could believe it. The whole scene was a sort of controlled chaos, like a travelling tornado, she thought. Exhilarating but slightly alarming as well. Unless you knew what you were doing, presumably. Which these people clearly did.

'They're very good.'

'You must tell Barbro. She thinks I don't treat it with proper respect.'

'You don't join in?' said Gaby, her eyes on the dancers, her blood pounding so hard, she thought those clever hands on her upper arms must feel it.

His hand tightenend. 'We can.'

She was so startled, she looked up at him. 'We?'

He smiled down at her. Her heart gave a great thump in her breast at the warmth in the grey eyes.

'Later. In some of the simpler dances. In fact that's what most of the people here will do.'

Gaby was breathless. 'But — I don't know what to do.'

He was looking at her mouth, his eyes hooded. 'I do.'

They were not, Gaby thought suddenly, talking about the dancing. She looked quickly away, transferring her attention back to the dancers. She shifted away from him slightly, disturbed as much by her own reaction as by the look in his eyes. But Sven pulled her back against his body. She could feel him laughing sound-lessly at her back. It did not calm her turbulent feelings but it did strengthen her resolution to hide them from him. She wasn't going to let him mock her. Not if she could help it.

The dancers stamped and whirled to their final close. There was a great shout of appreciation. Children surged forward to make up new sets for dancing. The circle was broken.

Gaby took the opportunity to detach herself from Sven's hold with as much composure as she could muster.

'Thank you,' she said sedately. 'That was very interesting.'

She met his mocking look and, too late, realised that he would apply her comment to more than the dancing. She fought down a blush. It would be all too evident. In spite of the fact that it was nearly midnight, the sky was still a silvery grey. Sven would be able to see every doubt and suspicion that crossed her face in the too revealing light.

He laughed and touched her cheek fleetingly. 'Come and dance. Trust me.' Gaby looked at him dubiously. 'I won't let you get lost,' he promised. 'Or trodden on. I have years of practice at keeping my partners on their feet.'

He was as good as his word. And if Gaby feared that

he would use the dance to make his physical power over her public, she need not have worried. He was a good dancer and he clearly knew the elaborate patterns of the dance but his touch was light, even when she turned in the wrong direction and he had to correct her.

In fact his touch was almost impersonal. Nobody watching them would have detected that he had held her against him earlier as if he would never let her go, Gaby thought. She began to wonder if she had imagined it. But then she met his eyes as their bodies came together again in the figures of the dance and knew she hadn't. And that the impersonal touch was entirely for public display.

When he put a hand under her elbow and turned her gently towards the car, Gaby trembled. But she went with him.

They drove back in near silence. The trees were like stalking giants in the headlights. Although it still wasn't pitch-dark, Gaby had difficulty in making out the rough track. But Sven drove with the absolute assurance of a man who could do it blindfold.

She folded her hands together in her lap, trying to calm her beating heart. He sent her a long look.

'All right?'

'Yes.' It was not much more than a breath.

'Good.'

At the house he stopped and switched off the engine. They sat side by side for an instant, not speaking. Then slowly, almost reluctantly, it seemed to Gaby, Sven put out a hand.

Her heart jumped into her throat.

He ran the back of his hand down her cheek. She shivered at the sensation that shot through her whole body.

'You have no disguises, have you?' He sounded almost sad. 'You show everything. You know that?'

Gaby remembered that he didn't even know her real name or her true relationship to Michael Hyssop. Now it suddenly seemed shabby not to have told him earlier. She bit her lip.

'I'm not as transparent as you think——' she began, but he interrupted.

'If only you weren't.'

Gaby shook her head. 'I don't understand.'

'No?' He ran his hand down her cheek again as if he loved the feel of it. 'If you weren't, I could pretend that you're as streetwise as I am. Then we could do what we both want.'

She swallowed. 'What we both want?'

He turned her face towards him. In the daunting shadows Gaby couldn't make out his expression. She had the impression of strong emotion, barely curbed. But he wasn't saying anything. Even the tell-tale hands were still as a rock.

He feathered his thumb across her lower lip. 'You know,' he said. It wasn't a question.

Gaby felt her whole body turn towards him. It was as if she had lost any ability to tell it what to do, as if it were being pulled by an inescapable magnetism to face the man beside her.

They were touching, at shoulder and hip. He was warm and solid, the only reality among the shadows. Gaby leaned against him. Her head fell back.

Just for an instant he hesitated. And then his mouth was on hers. Her eyes closed as the shadows fused into a driving need that filled her consciousness to the exclusion of all else.

CHAPTER EIGHT

THE kiss was long and infinitely gentle. Gaby felt her whole body contract with longing. She held him to her with all her strength. She heard him draw a shaken breath. In the close confines of the car their breathing was tumultuous. She felt Sven's mouth against her hair, her throat, the tender skin below her ear.

All memories of Tim and his grasping hands evaporated as if they had never been. This man held her as if he treasured her. She turned her head, seeking his mouth.

'Love me,' she said soundlessly.

Sven's hold became convulsive. The next kiss was not gentle. Gaby was hardly aware of it, straining against him in fierce need.

Eventually he raised his head. She saw the glint of his eyes as he looked down at her.

'Don't let me do this.'

But Gaby was dazed with sensation.

'This is crazy,' he whispered. The note of laughter was still there but his voice was not entirely steady.

Gaby thought, He's as shaken as I am. 'Is it?' she asked, curling against him in delight.

'Yes, of course it is.' He was getting control of himself, resuming that cool, indifferent manner that put people at a distance and kept them there. 'I haven't made love in cars since I was a schoolboy.'

It was a shock. Whatever she had expected him to say, it was not that. Nor had she expected him to switch out of that deliriously sensuous mood so abruptly. She was still there herself, though she was coming rapidly back to earth.

Gaby struggled to sound normal. 'I've never made love in cars at all,' she retorted.

The look he gave her was rueful. 'You don't have to tell me that.'

For some reason that was hurtful.

'Do we have to stay in the car, then?' she flung at him. It was a challenge. They both knew it. Sven caught his breath. His eyes flickered.

'Don't say things like that,' he said raggedly.

Gaby was defiant. 'Like what?'

But he didn't answer. He was scanning her face in the silvery shadows. The indentations beside his mouth were suddenly deep and bitter.

Gaby said in a quick hard voice, 'As I see it you want to make love to me. You simply haven't got the courage to admit it.'

There was a taut silence.

'I thought I just had,' he said levelly.

She shook her head. Why are you doing this? something inside her said. But she was angry with him; really *angry*.

'Oh, no. You've told me to stop you. You've told me this isn't what you're accustomed to.' Her voice dripped contempt. 'It makes you too vulnerable, doesn't it? It takes you out of the driving seat for once. But you can't actually face up to saying, Gaby, let's make love. Beneath your dignity, isn't it?'

His eyes were hooded. He was looking at her with an expression that was almost grim. Gaby returned the look with open hostility.

'You don't know what you're talking about,' he said at last.

'Oh, but I do. I've been here for two weeks, don't forget. What else have I had to do but watch and learn?' She gave a soft laugh. 'And I have. I know you, Sven Hedberg. I know that you won't risk anything unless you're in absolute control.'

His nostrils flared. 'Nonsense.'

'No, it isn't. That's why you won't wait for your hand
tremor to clear up by itself. Your body has to obey you,
doesn't it? And you've been running away from me
because I won't play by your *rules*,' she flung at him.
'You can't deal with anything that doesn't have rules,
can you?'

He was very pale round the mouth. 'Your watching
and learning doesn't seem to have taught you much.'

Gaby swallowed. Why was she doing this? You would
have thought she was in love with the man, the way she
was shouting at him.

'Oh, but it has. It's taught me you can't deal with
relationships.'

'Oh, we're talking about relationships now?'

In love with him. No. Oh, no, please God, not that.
Not in love with this icy-hearted games player.

In spite of her inner turmoil, she met his eyes levelly.
It was a matter of pride to do so.

'Relationships are how you connect with other
people, Sven,' she said quietly. 'You can't just *read*
them, and then tell them what to do, as if they were
some damned computer program.'

He reached out and tilted her chin so that their eyes
met. His were black with anger in the shadows; hers
were full of a pain she barely understood.

'Can't read people?' His voice was soft. 'Oh, but I
can.'

She moistened suddenly dry lips.

'Sven —'

'For instance, I've been reading you rather accu-
rately, wouldn't you say?'

This was treacherous ground. Listening to her own
troubled breathing, Gaby suddenly knew that she
needed to get away from him fast. That spotlight
intelligence could see right through her if she gave him
the chance. See through her and use the knowledge,
calculatingly and deliberately, and then discard what
wasn't interesting. Which just might be her whole self.

She wrenched her chin away with a jerk that hurt her neck. 'You don't begin to read me,' she said coldly.

She flung herself out of the car, not waiting to hear his reply. In spite of the warmth of the day the house struck chill as she went indoors. Sven had told her they never locked doors in the region and she shivered. No intruder would want to invade this unfriendly house, she thought. In the strange light it was positively threatening.

She didn't pause to hear him come in. She ran up the stairs to her room without putting on the light. Once there she flung herself on the bed as if it was a sanctuary.

What had happened out there in the car? Gaby thought wretchedly. What had been happening between them since that first traumatic encounter? Why was he so dismissive of her? So cold and yet sometimes as urgent as a lover? And why did he have this effect on her?

She put a hand to her throat. There was no denying the effect. Her heart was racing. The blood was beating furiously as if she had been in an accident instead of his arms.

Gaby shuddered, remembering all too clearly how she felt in his arms. She had never felt like this even before Tim had done his work. She had felt as if her heart was being scooped out of her breast by the devil himself.

'What have I got myself into?' Gaby whispered out loud. She clasped her arms round herself, suddenly chill. The trouble was, she thought shakily, that Sven was not a boy. His kisses weren't those of a boy. Nor was the cool distancing of himself from her the moment she was aroused and vulnerable in his arms. He had an awareness of her reaction that spoke all too clearly of years of experience. He understood her reactions better than she did herself, Gaby thought painfully. The way he stayed in control of himself and her too was wholly adult.

In the distance she heard the stairs creak. At once she was tense. But Sven went straight to his room. She relaxed in relief — or she told herself it was relief. It still kept her awake through that strange silvery night. She tossed her head into an ache and her hair into a tangle as she re-ran the scene in the car over and over again. How could she have had so little pride, so little self-respect? How could she?

In the morning she was heavy-eyed and subdued. She went downstairs as soon as she decently could, thinking she would make coffee quietly and take it back to bed with her before Sven was awake.

But he was there before her.

Gaby stopped in the kitchen doorway, shocked. He was sitting at the kitchen table, an earthenware mug in his hands. His eyes were shadowed, turned inwards. He looked cold, remote and heartbreakingly handsome.

He seemed not to notice her at first. He was turning the mug round and round, not looking at it.

But it wasn't his abstraction that startled Gaby. Nor was it the fact that he was downstairs at five o' clock when she had hoped she could make her coffee unobserved. It was his appearance.

He looked as if he hadn't been to bed at all. His eyes were sunken, the red hair was shockingly rumpled and there was a line of stubble on his jaw. He looked like something wild that had come out of the forest.

Gaby realised with a start that she had never seen him anything other than immaculately shaved before. Even when he was fishing or hauling logs, dressed in jeans and trainers, with his hair all over the place, he had never had that look of complete abandon that she was seeing now.

She must have made some small sound because he looked up. Their eyes met; locked. Gaby became simultaneously aware that her hair was flowing loose

about her and that he was staring at it. She felt
something slide down her spine that felt like solid ice.
His eyes were empty.

She said in a high, unnatural voice, 'I'm sorry. I
didn't realise you were here. I wanted coffee. I
thought —— But if you've made some, I'll just take a
mug and go.'

Sven didn't reply.

Gaby thought with a little lurch of the heart, I don't
think he even knows who I am. She swallowed and
pushed her hair back over her shoulders, walking across
to the old range. His eyes followed her. There was no
expression in them at all.

She picked up the heavy pot. To her surprise it was
cold. How long had Sven been sitting there, nursing
cold coffee? She began to heat it up, deliberately
making a business of it so she didn't have to acknowledge the brooding presence behind her. She didn't want
to look at him.

For, even unshaven and silent, Sven Hedberg was
the most attractive man she had ever known, ever even
imagined. The thin, handsome face was uncommunicat-
ive but it stirred Gaby's pulses to riot. She watched the
cast-iron pot as if her life depended on it.

At last he moved. He pushed the mug aside. It
scraped across the wooden table with a sound like
thunder in the silence between them. Gaby jumped.
She fought to compose herself. Then he pushed back
his chair. It fell over with a crash. She whipped round
as if the sound were a gun shot.

He was still watching her. At her expression, his
mouth slanted in a smile that was not kind. Gaby felt
her mouth go dry under that smile. She braced herself
against the range as he came across to her in three
strides.

The grey eyes were intent. No, they were more than
intent, they were blazing. Meeting that expression, her

heart contracted as if a giant had taken it in his hand
and squeezed every drop of blood out of it.

'Coffee?' he said. 'Oh, I think we know better than
that.'

'Sven —— ' she said on a rising note. It was meant to
be a warning but it sounded, even to herself, all too
like panic.

What is happening to me? she thought feverishly.

'Curiosity get the better of you, darling?' he said —
and jerked her into his arms with a roughness that
made her cry out.

He was very angry. Even in her astonished alarm,
Gaby detected that. More than angry. He was shaking
with fury. His mouth devoured hers. His hands tangled
in her loose hair. He was not gentle.

She fought him strenuously. He had no right to use
her like that. No right to make her feel as if he was
hauling her heart out of her body.

His breath forced her own back in her throat. Gaby
detected brandy, gasping. So it hadn't been coffee in
that mug he had been twisting and twisting in his hands.
She tasted brandy on her tongue and something else:
the bitter metallic hint of blood. Was it his or her own?
With a strength she didn't know she possessed, she
wrenched herself away from him.

She didn't stop to argue. She pushed past him and
ran. Sven followed, silent-footed and fast. He caught
her at the top of the staircase, spinning her round to
face him. Her hair swung, entangling both of them.
Eyes blazing, he was almost unrecognisable.

Gaby's sharp indrawn breath was lost in the devasta-
tion of his kiss. He was ruthless. She beat her hands
against his chest. It felt like iron. Her action did nothing
to make him loosen his hold. He did not even see to
notice.

Her head began to swim. His mouth moved, left her
lips and travelled. She felt warmth on the tender skin
below her ear. Her eyes drifted shut. He was moulding

her limbs as if her body were a thing he had made himself and knew to its core. Her head fell back. She heard herself sigh. Without her having made a choice, it seemed, her body was giving itself into his care.

He gave her a soft laugh. The anger was gone as if it had never been. With a swift, unexpected movement he picked her up. Gaby's eyes jolted open. She stared at him, astonished at the sensations that were sweeping through her. He looked down at her in his arms. He didn't look astonished at all.

That was when Gaby realised with a slight shock that something deep inside her wasn't astonished either. A part of her, a dark, secret part, had been waiting for this from the first moment she had set eyes on him.

Sven bent his head and feathered a kiss across her parted lips. It was a light kiss, careless, confident. It spoke of total possession.

'Yes,' he said.

He took her to her own room. The sun blazed through the windows, catching the simple bed in a net of light, barred with the reflected divisions between the window-panes. It had the oddest effect of distorting the sense of dimension. As he walked towards the bed with her held against his chest, Gaby felt as if she was floating in space and time. She fell back among last night's tumbled pillows with a little sigh of acceptance. This was right. This was where she should be. This was where she had wanted to be, in her unacknowledged dreams. This was where she had always known she would be in the end.

She reached up to him.

So she found that Sven Hedberg was un unhurried lover. He touched her gently, slowly, with infinite care until she was crying out to him, twisting and turning in a desire that was almost agony. Even when she arched, reaching for him, he would still not be hurried, soothing her with deft strokes of mouth and fingers until she felt her desire deepen and spiral beyond imagining.

And all the time he watched her. His eyes were hooded, unreadable; but he watched her intensely. His whole body was concentrated only on her. And in spite of that absolute physical control he was trembling.

Gaby heard herself make a small animal sound of pure craving. Her eyelids fluttered open. In the brilliant light his hair turned to fire. The strong, beautiful body seemed cast out of bronze. Gaby saw it through half-closed eyes, marvelling. Wonderingly she stretched out to run her hand up his arm and over the miraculous symmetry of his shoulder. Against that compact strength, her fingers felt fragile, weightless as butterflies.

Sven swallowed. She saw his throat move. The muscles of his shoulder contracted under her delicate touch.

'Love me,' Gaby whispered achingly, as she had done last night.

This time he didn't tell her to stop him. He looked down at her, his eyes like flames. He seemed to gather himself. For a single moment, as he held them both poised in suspense, Gaby had a fleeting terror that he was going to call a halt. Her fingers closed convulsively on the bones of his shoulder in instinctive protest at that anticipated denial, and with a wild cry that shocked her he moved over her in stark explicit need.

The need was mutual. Gaby was nearly frantic. She writhed against him, her hands clumsy on that smoothly muscled back. Sven, she found, was beyond control now. The slow, careful delight was gone as if it had never been. He was no longer watching her, tracing her every response to him. His eyes were fixed on her own now. Their expression was almost savage, as he drove his body inside hers. Gaby sobbed, binding him to her ferociously.

The spiral of sensation flung her higher and higher. She was blind and breathless. It was like a typhoon, she thought. She was terrified and yet she knew the storm

mustn't stop, couldn't stop. She needed. . . She
needed. . .

She heard Sven cry out. It was one of the loneliest
sounds she had ever heard. She wanted to find him in
whatever dark place he had reached; to assure him he
wasn't alone.

But she was trembling on the brink of dissolution,
her whole body shaking to pieces with the feelings he
had brought her to. Even as she reached out to Sven,
sensation took over. She could do nothing about it.
Gaby felt her eyes screwed tight, tight shut and she
exploded into a million particles of white heat. From a
long way away, it seemed, she heard her own voice
crying out as he had done.

There was a long, long silence. In the silence Gaby
came slowly back from the outer reaches of the galaxy
to find that she still had a body. The body was tingling
in every nerve and muscle. It was also barred with
sunshine and very warm — particularly where it was
pinned down by another body.

Gaby's eyes flew open. The brilliant light dazzled her
just for a moment. But in less than a second she realised
where she was. And what had happened. Her heart
lurched.

'Sven,' she said hoarsely.

The burnished head collapsed into her pillow did not
move. He was so close she had to narrow her eyes to
bring the tumbled hair into focus. She wanted to touch
it. The grey wing at his temple was an invitation. She
gave a deep shiver and her fingers curled at the thought.

'Sven,' she said again, more gently.

At that he stirred. Gaby could not prevent herself
wincing as the big body shifted across her. He must
have felt it because he turned his head sharply.

His eyes met hers. They were no longer far-away,
shadowed or inscrutable. They were all too easy read.
Sven Hedberg, realising where he was and with whom,
was quite straightforwardly horrified.

Gaby would not have believed anything could hurt so much. She shut her eyes, desperate to shut out that appalled expression.

Obviously he had been elsewhere in his imagination. After a sleepless night, God knew how much brandy and the provocation that she had seemed to offer him this morning, he had simply forgotten who she was and why she was here. He had been deep in his own thoughts and, when she'd intruded unexpectedly into his dawn reverie, he had reached for her as if she had a role in them.

Gaby wondered desolately who the lady was whose part she had taken. Serena Weissman? Whoever she was, she thought in pain, Sven must love her very much to look like that. As if he had betrayed the one true love of his life. She turned her head away.

Sven rolled off her and sat up. His breathing was harsh. Gaby could hear it in the silent room. She could hear him fighting for control as well. At last he said in a grim voice, 'An apology isn't much use. But for what it's worth, I'm sorry.'

This was worse even than she had thought. Bitterness flooded into her mouth. She folded her lips tight. Her eyes ached with tears. But with a bit of luck, Gaby thought carefully, she could suppress them until she was alone.

She was lost in a forest of feeling and badly hurt but one thing was clear: Sven Hedberg must not be allowed to know how badly he had hurt her. He must never be allowed to suspect even for a minute.

He said sharply, 'Gaby? Are you all right?'

It demanded an answer. Gaby swallowed the acrid taste in her mouth and managed a smile. She turned her head. She couldn't quite manage to look at him but she unfocused her eyes so that her vision skimmed the top of his head, and hoped he would think she looked dazed with pleasure.

'I'm fine.'

'You don't look fine,' he said critically. 'You look as if you've walked into a wall.'

And haven't I done exactly that? Gaby thought painfully. The wall of your indifference. But she went on smiling, her mouth stretched in an imitation of pleasure. He must never know what a travesty that expression was.

'You're imagining it.'

'Am I?'

The frowning look he gave her was searching. Gaby withstood it as best she could but she could feel her resolution weakening. If he carried on looking at her like that she would forget all dignity, her need to hide her hurt, and fling herself into his arms again. Beg him to carry on pretending that she was whoever the lucky woman was that he really wanted.

She ran her tongue round dry lips. 'Of course. I probably look tired. I didn't sleep well.'

His eyes flickered.

'I expect I could sleep now,' she said with a little artificial laugh, her eyes not meeting his.

Sven shook his head slowly.

'Are you telling me to go?'

Gaby winced at the wry question. But she kept her face calm.

'Not *telling* you.'

He gave a sudden harsh laugh. 'All right. You've made your point.' He pushed both hands through his hair, grimacing. 'Maybe you're right at that. We could both do with some space, I guess.'

'Yes.' Gaby's throat hurt with the effort of holding in the tears.

Sven swung himself off the bed. He looked down at her for a moment, brows knit. Gaby resisted the urge to fumble the coverlet round her. He was magnificently untroubled by his nakedness.

No doubt this was a familiar scene to him, Gaby thought, with a flicker of anger. She held on to the anger. At least it was normal. At least she had felt it before. At least it made for some healthy heat in the frozen waste that seemed to be her heart.

'All right. I'll leave you to sleep if that's what you want.' He paused. Gaby said nothing. He sighed faintly.

'But you and I are due a long frank talk, Gabrielle Fouquet.'

Gaby repressed a shudder. The last thing she could afford to do was talk frankly to Sven Hedberg. He was altogether too clever for her to risk that. Not if she was going to get out of this with any semblance of self-respect intact.

She feigned a huge yawn. Why wasn't he going? She decided to speed him on his way.

'Oh, no post-mortems, please.'

Sven went very still. Gaby's eyes slid away from him.

'After all, we're both adults,' she said with a desperate attempt at sophistication. Even to her own ears it sounded hollow. 'This isn't a first for either of us. . .' She stopped with a gasp.

He was bending over her, one muscled arm on either side of her, forcing her back among the pillows. Gaby swallowed.

'You're wrong,' he said softly.

She bit her lip. But she wasn't surrendering to intimidation. 'I told you. I'm not a child.'

He put out a hand and forced her head up. Gaby gritted her teeth but there was nothing else for it. He was compelling her to meet his eyes. She glared at him, hoping he would see the hostility and miss the lurking tears.

His eyes were grey and cold as pack-ice.

'I wasn't talking about you. I was talking about me.'

'*What*?'

'I've never done anything like this before,' Sven Hedberg told her, his jaw tight.

Gaby had the feeling that he was furiously angry.

'Oh, come on,' she protested. 'There have been dozens of women in your life. Everyone says so. And you as good as told me so yourself.'

For a moment she thought he was going to hit her. She shrank back among the pillows at the murderous expression on the thin, handsome face. Then he straightened abruptly.

'Other women, yes. I, however, don't regard the partners in my life as freely interchangeable.' His eyes were contemptuous. 'Unlike you, apparently.'

Gaby gasped. But before she could answer he had scooped his clothes off the floor in one angry movement and was gone.

She watched him go with a look of blank dismay. All the anger and the insults made no difference. What she had been afraid of all the time had happened. She had been right in the car last night. She was in love with Sven Hedberg.

CHAPTER NINE

SHE got up.

'Oh, my God, what have I done?' said Gaby aloud, pausing in front of the looking-glass.

Her face looked pinched and wretched. Her chin was as pointed as a witch's, she thought, her eyes bruised. She certainly didn't look like a woman who had just spent a heart-stopping hour in the arms of her lover.

'That's because he is not your lover,' Gaby told her mirrored self. 'You're in love. He isn't. He's made it clear from the start that he wants you making no claims on him. That's what you agreed. You can't back out now.'

In the end she went and showered and changed. She chose a print skirt, full and mid-calf length, and a long-sleeved T-shirt with a high neck. It felt like camouflage. Lifting her chin a fraction, she went downstairs.

This time there was a smell of coffee.

Oh, my God, Gaby realised. The coffee-pot. I left it on.

She rushed into the kitchen in a panic. Sven looked up from the range. She stopped dead.

He too had changed. He was back in jeans again, though these were black, and he had thrown on a dark green shirt. The colour made his hair look like a forest fire, Gaby thought, her mouth drying. Those grey wings at the temples were like cinders.

He gave her an unsmiling look. 'It's all right. I turned off the range. This hasn't double boiled.' He picked up the pot. 'Want some?'

Gaby couldn't find her voice. She wanted so badly to have the right to cross to him and have his arm round

her that it was like a physical pain. Subdued, she
nodded acceptance.

He poured some coffee into a mug for her and pushed
it across the table in her direction. He was very careful
that their fingers did not touch. Gaby bit her lip and
seized the coffee.

It was too strong and too hot. She burnt the roof of
her mouth, gulping the liquid down too quickly. She
would have given anything for milk. She would have
given anything not to be in this kitchen in a strange
house in the middle of nowhere with a cool and hostile
stranger to whom she had just made passionate love.
With whom she was in love, God help her.

I must get out, thought Gaby. I must get out *today*.

'Did you sleep?'

He could be a polite host, asking after the welfare of
an unfamiliar visitor, Gaby thought in despair. Her
voice still eluded her. She shook her head.

'Never going to speak to me again, Gabrielle?' he
sounded weary. 'Well, you have justification enough,
God knows. But it's not very practical.'

Gaby's heart shrank in her breast at the careful
indifference. She pulled herself together.

'Of course I'm still speaking to you,' she said in a
level voice. 'I just burnt my mouth on the coffee, that's
all.'

He tilted his head as if he didn't believe her, but he
didn't challenge it. He went to the window and propped
himself against it. The strong body was outlined by the
sun flooding in. Gaby felt her fizzing reaction like a jet
stream in the blood. Hastily she looked away.

'So what's your excuse for not looking at me?' Sven
said drily. 'Steam got in your eyes?'

Gaby's eyes came up defiantly at that. 'You're imagining things.'

'Am I?' He surveyed her, his expression enigmatic.
'That wasn't supposed to happen, you know, Gabrielle.
I didn't plan it.'

'I know.' There was a constriction in her throat. She swallowed hard. 'You even warned me off. Several times. I'm sorry I forgot.'

He uttered an expletive she didn't recognise, then, 'Don't be ridiculous,' he said curtly.

'You even told me to stop you,' Gaby said, turning the knife in her own wound. 'Last night. I should have listened.'

Sven closed his eyes briefly. The grooves beside his mouth were shockingly deep. He looked like a man in pain.

'I didn't give you any chance at all to stop me,' he told her brutally. He opened his eyes and looked at her straightly. 'There's no need for either of us to pretend. I know all too well what happened up there, what I did to you. I wish to God I didn't.'

Gaby sat up straight. 'I participated,' she said with great dignity.

A long-fingered hand dismissed her participation as of no account. Her heart became a small, hard pebble.

'I gave you no choice. You are not very old and much too trusting. While I — have had more experience than I could wish in these matters.'

The anger was beginning to come back. Thank God for anger. Gaby's chin lifted even higher.

'Are you trying to say that I have no will of my own? Or an instrument maybe, like one of those fiddles yesterday? Something which you can make play any damn tune you please.' Her voice was rising perilously.

'I think of you——' He stopped abruptly. 'We will not go into that.'

'Oh, won't we?' said Gaby, thumping down her mug so violently that coffee jumped out of it. She stood up and glared at him. 'Well, let me tell you, the truth is. . .'

'The truth,' said Sven in a quick hard voice, 'is that I knew what I was doing and you didn't.'

He couldn't have silenced Gaby more completely if he had slapped her.

He drew a long breath. 'I'm sorry,' he said, surprising her. 'I didn't mean to say that. I'm doing this all wrong. I meant — look, Gabrielle, you and I — I shouldn't have made you come here. I see that now. Something like this was bound to happen. As soon as I realised you had reservations, I ought to have sent you home. I shouldn't have — '

'Reservations?' interrupted Gaby, furious.

'About me. About sex in general.'

'*Reservations*?'

'About men, damn it.' Suddenly he looked as angry as she felt. 'After what that damned violinist did to you, you have every right to be wary.'

'Tim? You have the gall to talk to me about Tim?' Gaby was beside herself.

What had Tim to do with this hurricane she and Sven had called up between them? Tim had been a little drunk, a little greedy and highly determined not to hear the messages. He had hurt her a little and shocked her a great deal and it was all a long time ago.

This was now. It was terrible. It was making her heart bleed. But anger was a great pain-killer. Later she would be in agony, she knew. But now she was telling the truth with reckless determination.

'At least Tim didn't try to apologise,' she said with contempt.

Under the healthy tan, Sven whitened. Their eyes clashed like duellists. Gaby waited. But he said nothing. In the end he shrugged. Gaby turned and walked out of the house.

She wandered for miles through the trees. To begin with she was too blinded by tears to see any paths. Later she didn't care.

She crashed through the undergrowth, too absorbed in her spinning thoughts to mark where she was going. How dared he? Oh, how dared he? He had stripped

every last secret from her, every single inhibition. Then
when she was naked and wholly his he had *apologised*.
Oh, she would get away. She would make him grovel.
She would never see him again.

It occurred to her suddenly that she was going to
have difficulty in making Sven Hedberg grovel if she
was never going to see him again. She stopped and
dropped on to a discarded pine log. She gave a watery
sniff. But she was no fool and she could see how
ridiculous she was being.

No other man, Gaby thought bitterly, had ever
robbed her of her common sense along with her self-
control.

But common sense was reasserting itself now. She
began to look around for signs of a track. With a little
jerk of alarm she began to realise how far she had
strayed from the lake shore. She stood up and looked
about her, trying to get her bearings from the sun.

The place was completely still. High, very high above
her head, she thought she heard birds twittering. But
there was no other sign of them. The ground beneath
her feet was made up of fallen leaves and pine cones of
several winters. There was nothing to show that human
feet had trodden here before.

Gaby put a hand to her side to quell the leap of
alarm.

'Concentrate,' she said to herself fiercely. 'It's not so
long since you left the house. Think back. When did
you leave the edge of the lake? You climbed. You're
out of breath and the backs of your legs ache. How
long have you been climbing?'

But she had not put on her watch before she had
gone down-stairs looking for coffee. After Sven had
made love to her she had not been thinking clearly. It
must still be on the dressing-table.

She had no idea of the time, she realised. Or how
long it had taken her to get here. Or where she was.

A twig snapped in the forest behind her and Gaby

jumped. Were there still bears here? She searched her
memory frantically and could not remember. She had
heard there were elk and roedeer. She tried to convince
herself that neither animal was fierce, but she backed
nervously against a sturdy pine all the same.

After a while, when there were no more snapping
twigs, she came away from the security of the comfortable trunk. For a moment she considered climbing it.
Then she looked ruefully at her hands. They were the
only things that a pianist needed to protect, she
thought. She could not risk them clambering up trees.
The pine did not look particularly climbable, anyway.

She tried to locate the sun. Above the tops of the
pines the sky was almost painfully bright. But she had
no idea from which direction the brightness was
coming.

Move, she adjured herself. 'You can't wait till the
sun goes down to find out which is the west.

After a little thought she decided to carry on up the
slope. There might be a vantage-point at the top from
which she could get her bearings, she reasoned.

She did not know how long she walked. Several times
she heard little animals scuttle away at her presence.
But she saw nothing. And no bear surged out of the
trees to attack her. She got a stitch in her side, walked
on, and walked through it. She began to feel very tired
and hopeless.

Eventually she found herself on a ridge of sorts. The
tree cover was less dense here. She could make out in
the distance the mountains where Sven had told her he
had climbed. She calculated carefully. If the house were
the centre of a dial and the mountains looked as if they
were at the figure ten from the house and now they
looked as if they were at the figure three. . . She turned
slowly, stretching an arm out ahead of her to mark her
imagined path. It led down into the forest again, away
from the ridge.

'Mother had better be right,' Gaby muttered. 'If the

Lord doesn't provide, I seem to be due a night in the forest. On my own.'

She set off reluctantly. It was very warm. Even in the shadow of the trees Gaby was soon uncomfortably hot again. Several times she stumbled. Once she started through a thicket which got denser and denser, with branches plucking at her loose hair and snaking across the bare flesh of her arms, leaving little blooded tears on her soft skin.

'It's to be hoped there aren't any vampire bats as well,' Gaby said out loud, retreating.

She would have to find a way round the thicket even if she risked losing the fine straight line she had set herself. She also bound her hair into a rudimentary plait, to keep it away from the prickly twigs.

She walked through the heat of the day. From time to time she stopped but all she saw was the calm, indifferent forest. Then the light changed to the pro-longed silvery twilight. Gaby began to feel seriously concerned.

And then she heard it: a little steady rushing noise.

'A stream,' she said.

She was no woodsman but she knew that if she found a stream and followed its downward path she was likely to come to the lake eventually. Well, a lake, she amended, ironically. She might have walked into the territory of another lake by now. She had no idea how much territory she had covered in her blunderings.

It was a little waterfall. At some point someone had built up a platform beside it. The logs were rough but they were clearly set there by design. And there was a small square notice pegged into the ground beside it. It was in Swedish, of course, so she had no idea what it said. But it looked like a label plus a few lines of narrative.

It had to be a sign on one of the nature trails Sven had talked about, Gaby thought. It had to be. And

where there were nature-trail labels there was a path to
somewhere.

Now that she had found a path she realised how
frightened she had been. She sat down rather shakily
and let the spray play on her hot face.

The path was easier walking. No more brambles
plucked at her hair and arms, no more hidden dips
turned her ankles. But it was steep in places. And she
was ferociously tired. More than once she nearly sat
down. It was only the thought of Sven's unsurprised
contempt if she did that kept her going.

In the end, rather desperately, she started to sing.
Which was how she surprised the man in the bushes.
Well, two men. She heard them talking just a couple of
seconds before one of them erupted on to her path, a
startled expression on his face.

Gaby stopped in consternation, a Mozart march
dying on her lips. It was Anders Storstrom.

'Good heavens! Miss Hyssop.' He looked uneasily up
and down the path. 'And where is my good friend the
doctor?'

Gaby remembered that last night his good friend the
doctor had thrown him into the lake. She denied any
knowledge of his whereabouts.

'I just went along the nature trail,' she said airily.
'Went further than I meant, to be honest.'

'Ah,' said Storstrom with an unpleasant leer, 'some
young ladies seem to do that with the good doctor.'

Gaby decided that Sven had been quite right to throw
Storstrom into the lake. She opened her eyes wide,
however, and said innocently, 'But he wasn't with me.
He was working.'

An expression of distinct annoyance came over
Storstrom's face. He looked quickly behind him into
the bushes.

'In fact I'm not even sure which way I should go to
get back to the house,' Gaby said with honesty.

'You didn't take a map?' Storstrom was sneering.

Gaby wondered wistfully if Sven might throw him
into the lake again. Or if she might even manage it for
herself. But she gave an empty-headed laugh and said
truthfully, 'I didn't think I would be out so long.'

Storstrom looked at her narrowly. Then he shrugged.
'It is not so far. I will escort you, if you permit.'

Gaby wished she could have said no. But the house
was still not in sight and her trail-finding had not been
distinguished.

'Thank you,' she said prettily, despising herself.

'Come, then.'

In fact she hardly needed his escort. The path was
almost on the flat now. It got wider and wider, unmistakably winding down to the lake itself. Gaby was
almost running along it when she heard her name
called.

Storstrom stopped. A curious expression crossed his
face. Once again he looked behind him.

'My friend the doctor,' he said loudly. 'He seems to
be worried.'

Sven appeared. He was not on the path but the steep
hillside above it. Gaby saw him an instant before he
leaped lightly down in front of them.

Storstrom recoiled as if he were being ambushed. His
expression of unease deepened. Sven ignored him. He
strode towards Gaby, frowning.

'Are you all right?' he asked her harshly.

Storstrom stepped forward. 'Of course.' It was
smooth. 'Miss Hyssop has been with me.'

Sven checked his stride imperceptibly. Then he
reached Gaby and took her by the arm, turning it so
that her injuries were evident. In the twilight the
scratches were ugly and oozing.

'You don't seem to have taken very good care of
her,' Sven said levelly.

'I did that up on the ridge.' Gaby was breathless. To
her disgust she sounded almost guilty. 'I've only just
bumped into Mr Storstrom.'

'Really?' Sven was cool.

Gaby nodded. 'I found the nature trail by accident and followed the stream. . .' Her voice died away. She looked into his eyes. Not cool. Sceptical.

'And came back to me, stopping off only for a brief editorial conference *en route*. Understandable in the circumstances.' The soft voice bit.

Gaby stared.

Storstrom said hastily, 'Well, I must be getting back. Can't keep dinner waiting.' He nodded to her. 'Glad to have put you on your way, Miss Hyssop. Goodnight, Doctor.'

He almost ran back up the path.

'Goodnight,' Gaby said to his retreating back. She felt at a loss.

She turned to Sven. For some reason her eyes stung with tears. Ruthlessly she brought them under control. She said clearly, 'I got lost. I was upset. I walked into Mr Storstrom less than five minutes ago.'

He stood watching her, his expression unreadable. He made no move towards her.

'Did you tell him?' Sven asked eventually.

Gaby was confused. 'Tell him what?'

His mouth moved in distaste. 'What happened this morning.'

She gasped. She could feel the colour draining out of her face. Her eyes ached with the tears. This time she couldn't control them.

'No, I didn't,' she shouted at him. The tears fell embarrassingly fast. 'I wish I had. I hate you,' she added on a note that even she knew was childish.

His face looked as if it had been carved from marble. 'Perhaps you should have.'

Gaby dashed a hand across her eyes. 'I'm leaving,' she announced. She held her breath, waiting for him to contradict her, braced for battle.

But all he said was, 'Of course.'

'Now,' said Gaby, furious.

He looked at the sky. Now that she did not need it, of course the sun was very clear above the distant mountains.

'That's not very practical. I'll have to get you a seat on a flight to London and drive you to Stockholm. It all takes time.'

'I don't care,' Gaby said. 'I don't want to spend another hour in this house with you,' she added with loathing.

His jaw tightened. 'I appreciate that. Unfortunately neither of us has much choice.'

Gaby's control broke suddenly. 'Don't be so damned logical,' she shouted.

Sven's jaw set. 'One has to be practical.' He paused and then added with lethal precision, 'Miss Hyssop.'

And suddenly Gaby realised.

'Oh, lord,' she said, the picture of guilt.

'Or is it Mrs Hyssop?' he asked in a neutral voice.

Gaby winced. 'Michael is my father,' she said.

He inclined his head. 'I see.'

'I don't know why I let you think anything else,' she muttered. 'It was stupid. Only you made me angry. It seemed like protection of a sort, I suppose.'

He gave a mirthless laugh. 'Protection! Not very effective, was it?' Gaby knit her brows. 'Bearing in mind what happened this morning,' he added deliberately.

Her flush was vivid and immediate. She looked away.

He said quietly, 'Gabrielle, will you tell me something?'

She was still fighting to control her painful blush. 'What?' She did not sound encouraging.

'Did you really meet Storstrom on the plane? Or did you do your deal with him before you ever came out to Sweden?'

Gaby's mouth fell open. 'Did my deal?'

Sven nodded in the direction of the bushes. 'The gentleman in the undergrowth with the zoom lens.'

Gaby remembered the hurried conversation she had heard before Anders Storstrom had stepped on to the path.

'What's he doing there?'

'I think we can dismiss the possibility that he is photographing the autumn migration,' Sven said drily. 'Especially as he has had his lens firmly sighted on the house all day.'

'The house? Your house?'

'Oh, please,' he said, suddenly impatient. 'You know as well as I do. You clearly share your father's taste for publicity.'

Gaby shook her head, the brown fronds escaping from her plait in increasing confusion.

'I don't know what you're talking about.'

'No?' He laughed. 'And yet you ran straight from me to Storstrom this morning. Did you write the story yourself, or is he having it ghosted?'

This was a nightmare. Gaby was so tired she was swaying on her feet. But the very force of his anger seemed to keep her upright. She said, 'You're wrong.'

'Am I? I don't think so, darling.'

She shut her eyes. 'Sven, please believe me——' Gaby was swaying in earnest now. Sven steadied her with an impersonal hand. In the split-second before she recognised the impersonality of his touch, she dropped her head on to his shoulder with a sigh of relief. She had come home.

He went very still. She realised, too late, that the arm around her was not holding her against him. Her face flaming, she made to draw away. But he did not let her. Instead his arm tightened. Looking up, she saw that the ice-grey eyes were blazing.

'Your friend want some better shots?' he said. His mouth was smiling like a tiger that had scented dinner. Only his mouth was smiling. His eyes were wild. 'Look happy, then, darling. You're having your picture taken.'

He bent his head and subjected her to a long kiss. The insult was blatant and deliberate.

Gaby fought herself away from him, eyes darting fire. 'I'm going to make you sorry for that, Sven Hedberg,' she choked. 'I'm going to make you *grovel*.'

She flung herself away from him down the path. She ran across the bridge and into the house without looking back. In her room she flung clothes into her bag, her hands shaking.

Sven appeared in the doorway, his expression glacial. 'I've got you a flight. Tomorrow evening.' His voice was clipped.

'Thank you.' Gaby was chilled. 'Have you ever been in love?' she asked at last, bitterly, knowing it was unwise, knowing she had nothing to lose.

Sven looked at her for a long unspeaking moment, then said, 'More material for your article? Sven Hedberg confesses.' He was contemptuous. 'No, I've never been in love.'

For some reason—she had no idea why—Gaby did not quite believe him.

He said suddenly, 'Let me tell you something, Gabrielle Hyssop. When you see your photograph in the gossip columns you may remember it. My sister Elisabeth had been reading about her marriage in Anders Storstrom's paper the day before she died.'

Gaby gasped. The harsh, beautiful face was bitter with memories.

'God knows why those two got married in the first place. When he got tired of dewy-eyed devotion, Mats went back to playing the field. Elisabeth stayed home playing house—until Storstrom printed a picture of Mats leaving his girlfriend's flat one morning.'

'It was an accident. . . At least that's what they called it,' Barbro had said.

So this was why he hated newspapers, hated them printing stories about himself, hated and despised her father for that silly piece of news in the Hollywood

Press. Gaby felt sick. She made a helpless gesture. 'I'm sorry,' she said. She closed the lid of her suitcase and turned to face him. She said with quiet dignity, 'I know you're not going to believe me now. Perhaps you never will. But neither I nor my father ever gave any story to the Press about you. Everything I have said to you here, I have meant.'

'Love me,' she had said. She hoped he was not remembering that now. Though if he challenged her she would not deny it. The truth was too important between them now.

'Everything I have done here I have done because I — ' she looked at his flinty expression and her heart failed her. Truth or not, she could not face this ice man and tell him she loved him ' — wished you well.' She paused before saying gently, 'And if you ever see my photograph in the newspaper, you may even remember it.'

CHAPTER TEN

GABY didn't sleep. She lay with her ears strained for creaks on the stairs or the floorboards outside her room. None came. Sven appeared to be staying downstairs.

When she finally left her room the next morning there was no sign of him either. Barbro was in the kitchen, her long horse face alive with curiosity.

'He's spitting mad,' she informed Gaby without preamble. 'What on earth has been going on?'

Gaby swallowed something jagged in her throat. 'Nothing.'

Barbro snorted. 'You looked happy enough together at Midsummer Eve. What went wrong?'

'How do you know anything has gone wrong?' Gaby said. 'I came here to do a job. I might just have done it.'

'In which case he would be driving you to Stockholm himself instead of calling in the local taxi service,' Barbro said unanswerably. 'And biting my head off into the bargain.'

So Sven wasn't driving her to the capital. Maybe he wasn't even intending to say goodbye. Perhaps she had seen him for the last time. Gaby bit her lip.

'You must have really shaken him up,' Barbro said in congratulatory tones.

Gaby shook her head. 'Oh, no. He's angry with me but it's just temper, He'll forget.'

Barbro busied herself at the range. She was clearly bent on producing a breakfast worthy of the finest hotel in Sweden.

With her back turned to Gaby she said, 'Is that what you want him to do? Forget?'

Gaby gave a laugh that broke in the middle. Well, if she couldn't admit the truth to Sven at least she could do it to herself — and incidentally to Barbro.

'What I want him to do,' she said deliberately, 'is carry me off to that room you made up for us both and keep me there until he promises never to let me go as long as we live.'

Barbro put toast on the table. She seemed unaware of the magnitude of Gaby's confession. She even looked amused.

'Not quite Sven's style.'

Gaby looked down at her hands with a small, secret smile. It had nearly been, once. Then she sighed. 'I know. Or mine up to now.' She sat down at the table, surveying the feast before her without enthusiasm. 'I don't know what's come over me.'

Barbro put a large plate of thinly sliced ham and cheese on the table.

'Don't you?'

Gaby shook her head. 'Well, yes, I suppose I do, heaven help me.' A sudden anxiety assailed her. She looked pleadingly at Barbro. 'Don't tell him.' Then she sighed again. 'Not that he'd believe it anyway, I suppose.'

'Ah,' said Barbro. 'You're in love with him.'

Gaby winced. 'I'll get over it.'

I have to get over it, she told herself. He is never going to love me. He's never going to love anyone. He's made that perfectly clear. Particularly not me who lied to him. After last night it's clear he doesn't ever want to see me again.

She didn't say any of that to Barbro, of course. She didn't say any of it to her father, either, when she got back to England.

'I didn't manage to talk him out of the lawsuit,' she told Michael curtly. 'He wasn't listening to anything I said and anyway he didn't trust me. He didn't trust either of us.'

Michael was philosophical. 'Well, it was worth a shot. Thanks for trying, chicken. At least you made some money and had a bit of holiday out of it.'

Her mother was more perceptive. 'Didn't work?' she said.

As usual she was only briefly available between patients. She was tidying the consulting-room while they talked.

'The music?' Gaby was startled. She had almost forgotten her unrewarding attempt at therapy. 'No, it didn't. He didn't give it a chance.' Her voice was more bitter than she realised.

'Interesting,' murmured Anne. 'How long were you out there?'

'Two weeks, just over,' Gaby said absently, folding peach-coloured towels.

Anne smiled. 'He must have co-operated to begin with. Or you'd have come home.'

Gaby looked up. Under the otherworldly manner, Anne could sometimes prove surprisingly shrewd.

'He did the exercises. Reluctantly.'

'That's something.'

'Yes, but he never put his heart into it,' Gaby said.

Anne began to reorganise a tray of flower-remedy phials with absorption.

'So what did he put his heart into?'

'His work,' returned Gaby without hesitation.

Her mother raised her eyebrows. 'But I thought you said he couldn't work properly until his hand tremor was cured?'

Gaby dismissed it with a gesture. 'It wasn't incapacitating, just bad when he got tired. Anyway, he could still write notes telling other people what to do,' she said sourly. 'He likes telling other people what to do. So that's what he did. Every day.'

Anne laughed. 'You seem to have got to know him rather well.'

Gaby repressed a shiver. 'You could say that,' she said in a constrained voice.

'Will you be seeing him again?' Anne asked innocently.

'No!' It was explosive.

Anne's brows went even higher.

'Don't you want to know what happens next?'

Gaby's heart lurched. What had Anne detected?

'What do you mean? Nothing's going to happen next. It's finished. There's nothing between us. Nothing.'

Anne bit back a smile. 'I never suggested there was,' she said mildly. 'I just thought you might like to know whether his hand improves. After all your hard work. And whether he goes ahead with suing your father, of course.'

'Oh.' Gaby was silenced.

'It only seems human nature. Unless he hurt you so badly you never want to see him again,' Anne pursued, running her finger along the top of a bookshelf and inspecting it thoughtfully for dust.

Gaby was not taken in by the air of gentle abstraction. One way or another Anne had managed to draw the right conclusions. She bit her lip.

'How did you know?'

'Darling, I'm your mother. I know you think I'm vague but how could I miss it when my daughter fell in love?'

Anne laughed at her dubious expression. 'And your father phoned me,' she admitted. 'He was worried about you, he said you weren't yourself. I think he was afraid you'd quarrelled with the man.'

Gaby blenched, remembering. 'I did.'

'Of course,' said Anne serenely. She looked at her watch. 'I'm sorry to hurry you, darling, but I've got another consultation in three minutes. We could get together tomorrow evening if you want to talk.'

It was Gaby's turn to laugh. 'About my broken heart?' She shook her head. 'It's all right, Mother, I can get by without talking,' she said drily. 'Hearts mend. Or so I'm told.'

Walking home, she thought that she wished she had some evidence that it were true. Her heart showed no signs at all of mending. All too often she would find herself breaking off mid-practice, her hands still on the piano keys, her mind on the Swedish lakes. Half the time she was in a dream, turning over and over in her mind every single word he had ever said to her. Calling back every touch. Indulging herself in memory with delicious abandon until she would come back to the present with a start, to find herself bereft and alone.

The rest of the time she was violently active. She practised till the small hours. She worked on Christofsen's new piece until the wretched composer himself begged for mercy. She took on two new piano pupils. And then she would lapse into her reverie again and no one would be able to get any sense out of her. It went on for three months.

She played at In Camera four nights a week. The management were so pleased that she found a spring-green evening dress waiting for her one day when she arrived. They were surprisingly embarrassed when she thanked them. 'Thought you needed cheering up,' one of them volunteered eventually.

They were not the only ones who thought she needed cheering up. Her abstraction began to cause comment. Her flatmates decided charitably that she was working too hard. Her tutor, who knew all too well that she wasn't, had harsher things to say.

'If you don't get your head together, you'll find yourself suspended,' he told her brutally.

That shocked Gaby as it was meant to. 'But—but I'm playing all right, aren't I?' she said, scared.

'You're playing bloody brilliantly when you're play-ing. And you know it. The trouble is, nobody knows when you're going to turn up. I've given colleagues as

many excuses for your cutting their classes as I'm going
to. From now on you take your chances.'

Gaby took the warning to heart. It didn't stop her
lying awake, racked by painfully explicit memories of
being in Sven's arms, but it brought her back to the
reality of classes and term papers.

It didn't stop her jumping every time the telephone
rang either. Sven knew the number, after all. He could
call her at any time, she thought.

He didn't. He neither telephoned nor wrote. The
autumn recital season started and Gaby began to pick
up more work. Michael went back to Los Angeles.

Eventually the cheque that was due to her arrived. It
came via his secretary, routed through her father's
Beverly Hills office. There was a typed letter of thanks
accompanying it that was so formal Gaby felt she could
have burned her fingers on the icy page. So he had not
discovered that he was mistaken in thinking she had
been in league with Storstrom. That hurt. She tore up
the letter and thought wistfully of doing the same with
the cheque. But common sense prevailed. There were
the household bills to be met. And in spite of In
Camera's generosity, she had to buy a new dress for the
premier of the Christofsen. She needed that cheque.

She didn't like needing it, though. As some sort of
gesture against common sense, Gaby bought a dress
that was much too expensive, a defiant swirl of imperial
scarlet and purple that made Christofsen look distinctly
nervous. Even Anne opened her eyes wide at the
flagrant show-off.

'Challenging,' she said, a private smile hovering at
the corners of her mouth. 'Er—do you think the critics
will notice the music?'

'That's what I thought,' said David Christofsen
gloomily.

But he need not have worried. The reviews were
bordering on ecstatic. Gaby was the only one who was
surprised.

Surprised and rather flattened. After all the work and the tension before the concert, she felt strangely weepy and bad-tempered after it.

'Just as well that David's doing the media interviews,' she told her father ruefully. He was in London again, partly for the concert, partly on his own business. 'I'd bite their heads off.'

'What you want,' said Michael, 'is something to give your mind a new direction.'

Gaby flung up a hand. 'No,' she said. 'Whatever it is, no. The last time you gave my mind a new direction I —— ' She broke off, flushing suddenly.

'You?'

'Ended up in the middle of nowhere,' Gaby said with an effort at flippancy. The effort showed.

'Hmm,' mused Michael. 'Did you know he dropped the suit against me?'

Gaby nodded. Anne had told her. She had not felt able to grill her mother on the reasons for it, though. Quite apart from anything else, Anne would not have remembered them.

'Did he say why?' she asked after a pause. Her indifference was not much more convincing than her flippancy but her father forbore to comment.

'I assumed it was your intervention.'

'Oh, no,' Gaby said with absolute conviction.

'I think you may underestimate yourself,' Michael said, watching her. 'He spoke of you very highly.'

'Spoke? You've seen him?' Gaby was suddenly as tense as a coiled spring. 'Did he mention me?'

Michael shrugged. 'We bumped into each other. He seemed —— ' He hesitated. 'He seemed to think he had offended you,' he said, choosing his words with care. He looked at her searchingly. 'Seriously, I mean.'

Gaby winced. 'Did he?'

'What did he do, Gaby?' her father asked quietly. 'Whatever it was, it's eating him up.'

She looked away.

'He apologised to me, you know. He said that he had over-reacted to that news story and he knew it. Said he'd got it out of proportion because of something that happened a long time ago. He said — implied that you'd had a hand in giving him back his perspective.'

Gaby's only answer was a little laugh that broke in the middle.

Michael sighed. 'What happened, Gaby? Your mother's worried, you know. You've never been happy since you got back from Sweden, have you? That's why you don't care two hoots about this première. Any other girl would be walking on air. Six months ago you wouldn't have let Christofsen hog all the limelight. Now you don't seem to care about anything except playing the piano all hours God sends. It's not healthy at your age.'

Gaby said, 'That's because I was warned at the start of term about irregular attendance. Now I'm earning back Brownie points. That's all.'

Michael studied her. 'Why don't you go and see him?' he said unexpectedly.

Gaby jumped. 'See him?' she said in tones of unmistakable horror. Then, catching herself, 'See who?'

'So you do care about him,' her father diagnosed.

Gaby said carefully, 'I'm not sure what I feel for him.'

'Why don't you go and find out, then?'

'Because he doesn't want me,' she flared. 'He knows how to get in touch with me if he wants. He's even got my number, damn it.'

Michael said disapprovingly, 'That's very hidebound, not to say sexist. I'm disappointed in you, Gaby. I see no reason why you shouldn't go and see Sven Hedberg if you're eating your heart out for him. As you clearly are. No reason at all.'

No reason? When he thought she had lied and cheated? When he hadn't even been able to bear to see her on that last day?

Gaby began to laugh. It was a harsh, grating sound. It plainly startled her father. It rather startled her.

'Oh, but there is,' she said when she could speak. 'You have no idea.'

Her father let the subject drop but he looked concerned. But not, fortunately, concerned enough to engineer a meeting between Sven and herself, Gaby found. From his attitude she had half expected it. When he went off on the next leg of his European tour without doing anything about it, she didn't know if she was more relieved or wretched.

Luckily she didn't really have time to think about it. Offers to play the Christofsen round the world were beginning to pour in. Her agent was offered a recording contract and hesitated, trying to talk up the fee.

'You're a success,' David Christofsen told her.

Gaby smiled wryly. She didn't feel a success. She felt empty. As empty as her nights.

And then her agent phoned with another offer. Most of the concert engagements were booked a season ahead at least, but this was all immediate.

'A Christmas concert in one of the palaces,' her agent said. 'They were supposed to be having Czarnik's new quintet but he hasn't finished it. So they want the Christofsen to fill in. You can do it, can't you, Gaby?'

Her agent knew her schedule better than she did herself.

'If you say so,' Gaby said indifferently.

Which was why she found herself disembarking at Stockholm Airport again one cold winter's morning.

As soon as she'd realised the concert was in Sweden, she had protested. But by then it was too late.

Gaby looked round nervously, alert to her surroundings for the first time in months. But there was no tall auburn-haired man with icy eyes waiting for her. Instead there was a pleasant girl and a truly enormous bouquet of flowers.

The hotel was warm and comfortable. The city was a

magic place of lights and water. The palace was eight-eenth-century luxury at its most sumptuous and the audience was ecstatic. Gaby was in agony.

Every time someone called her name, it seemed as if her heart stopped. All through the performance she was shaking with nerves which had nothing to do with the music or the audience. This was his city and all day she had expected to see him at any moment.

She did not. She told herself she was glad.

After the concert there was a reception. Gaby would have cried off if David Christofsen hadn't taken her firmly by the arm into the waiting crowd.

The room was all delicate pastel furniture and gilded mirrors. The hum of the crowd was almost lost in the height of the gorgeously decorated ceiling. The scent of great troughs of hothouse lilies was almost overpowering.

Gaby accepted a tall glass of champagne and smiled gratefully at the compliments that were showered on her. Everyone spoke English as well as Barbro and Sven, she noticed. She told herself that it was interest-ing, not painful, to remember.

And then, as she stood momentarily alone in her scarlet dress, a voice behind her said, 'If I say you played wonderfully tonight, will you walk away from me again?'

Gaby went very still. It was the voice she had been waiting for since she'd got off that plane, she thought. It called to something in her very bones. Her hand began to tremble. Very carefully she put down her champagne glass and turned.

'Hello, Sven,' she said quietly.

Her eyes took him in hungrily. He was looking thinner, she thought. The lines by his mouth were great slashes as if he had been in pain or working ferociously. But his gleaming hair was unchanged and so was the cool, measuring expression in the storm-grey eyes. He was still the best-looking man in the room.

He also seemed to be alone. Gaby tried to look unobtrusively for the lady he had to be with. What was she called? Serena something? But there seemed to be no one.

He said, 'You're not walking away.'

'What?' She stared at him.

His mouth slanted wryly. The smile she remembered so well, had remembered all through the empty nights, made her heart lurch in her breast.

'I thought you weren't ever going to talk to me again.'

Gaby said, 'I thought that was mutual.' She added candidly, 'You were in a shocking temper. Even Barbro said so.'

The look of pain deepened the lines on the thin, handsome face.

'I was suffering from the worst conscience of my life. It tends to affect my temper. I hadn't,' he added with great deliberation, 'treated you very well. Barbro wasn't to know that, of course.'

Remembering what had happened before that final parting, Gaby flushed rosily. Her eyes fell. She murmured something inaudible.

'In fact for a lady who claims to have my interest at heart, Barbro made more mischief than I would have believed possible,' Sven said wryly. 'She told you I'd asked her to make up only the one bed, didn't she? As if I expected you to sleep with me from the moment you arrived.'

Gaby swallowed. 'Yes,' she muttered.

'I didn't know that until she told me,' he said reflectively. 'Of course, you weren't to know it wasn't true. She thought she was looking after your interests.' His eyes gleamed. 'Understandably. 'She could see what I wanted.'

Gaby looked up, surprised. 'It wasn't true? But Barbro didn't seem like a liar.'

'She isn't. She's a good motherly soul who thought

you needed looking after.' He sighed. 'She told me at once, when you'd gone.' His voice deepened. 'Along with one or two other things.'

Gaby bit her lip. Had Barbro told him that Gaby wished Barbro's well meant lie had been fulfilled?

When she did not speak, he went on, 'I taxed her with making mischief, once you'd gone and I was thinking straighter. She admitted it. Apparently you weren't taking her warnings seriously enough. So she decided to bend the truth a little.'

'Oh.' Gaby digested that. 'Why?'

'She thought you were very young. And vulnerable.' He looked away suddenly, his expression bitter. 'She was right.'

Gaby glared at him. 'I wish you'd stop talking about me as if I'm just out of the cradle. I shall be twenty-five next month, which, let me tell you, technically makes me an old maid.'

'*What*?'

'If you're over twenty-five and still unmarried on Saint Katherine's Day you're an old maid,' Gaby told him with a hint of smugness. 'Which I shall be. Shirley Temple I'm not. In fact I'm on the shelf, if you look at it in one way.'

He laughed suddenly. His eyes warmed and the painful lines dissolved in real amusement. Amusement, she thought, her heart stopping — and affection?

'I don't think so,' he said.

The amusement died out of the face but the warmth remained. Something hurt and jagged inside Gaby began to heal quite suddenly.

'Sven——'

He looked down at her. 'Yes?'

People jostled them. Someone congratulated her. Gaby smiled, not seeing them. They moved away, leaving her in a cocoon of quiet with Sven.

'Why did you send me away like that?' she asked in a low voice.

His eyes darkened at once as if she had touched a wound. But he said steadily, 'I knew what I had done. I was no better than that boy who hurt you.' He shut his eyes briefly. 'He raped you, didn't he? You never quite said it. But I knew. And I'd done the same.'

'No,' said Gaby on a shocked breath.

He shook his head, the auburn lights in his hair turning to pure gold under the gleam of the chandelier. 'Don't be kind to me, Gaby. I knew what I was doing. I knew you——' He broke off abruptly wincing. 'You ran away from me up that staircase and I went after you like a hunter. You were terrified.'

Gaby put a hand on his arm. 'No. It wasn't like that. I was afraid, I admit it, but not of you, of *me*. Of what I was feeling. I didn't think you felt anything for me at all. You'd already asked me if I'd feel better if you pretended to be in love with me, do you remember that? I was desperate for you not to pretend. By that time I knew I was in over my head. Yet I didn't think you could feel anything real for me.'

He groaned, his hands going out to her. 'Real. Dear God.'

'Sven, wonderful to see you,' someone said.

Sven nodded, his face impatient.

'Marvellous playing,' someone else said.

'Another glass of champagne, madam?'

'This is too much,' Sven said under his breath. He placed a hand under her elbow and steered her masterfully towards a doorway with a velvet curtain looped across it.

'We can't. It's private,' Gaby said, shocked, as he turned the handle and ushered her through it.

'I devoutly hope so,' Sven said grimly, letting the curtain fall back into place behind them. He closed the door and set his shoulders against it. 'Come here, my darling.'

It was a long, shattering kiss.

When she could breathe again, Gaby found that her

elegant coiffure had been ravaged. Sven was stroking
long chestnut strands over her shoulders and down her
arms. She shivered in sensuous delight.

He turned his face in her hair. 'Oh, God, I thought
I'd never do this again,' he said in a shaken voice. 'That
last day—you looked so hurt. Even when I was shouting at you I kept thinking, This is crazy. She's not like
this. She's gentle and she trusts too much. But when I
saw you with Storstrom I just went a bit crazy. He is
everything I loathe. I'd just found his spy, too. And it
seemed as if you knew they were there. Oh, my darling,
I know I was cruel but I felt so betrayed. Can you
understand that?'

She touched his face. 'It was partly my own fault. I'd
been playing silly games, not telling you my real name,
letting you think I was Michael's girlfriend.'

He held her away from him, looking down into her
face with so much love in his expression that Gaby
barely recognised him.

'Yes, that was a major problem. Why did you do it?'

She shivered a little. His arms tightened.

'I'm not really sure. I—it seemed as if you got to me
so, so *easily*. It frightened me. When you jumped to
that conclusion I sort of went along with it as a kind of
defence. It sounds stupid, I know.'

'No. Not stupid. I was trying to defend myself too,'
Sven said into her hair. 'The first time I saw you, I was
shocked. I thought, She's mine. I'd never thought that
before. Never imagined it. Then I saw you playing in
that restaurant and flirting with Hyssop—as I thought—
and I was furious. I thought you ought to have recognised that you belonged to me. I did.'

Gaby shook a dazed head. 'That soon? But you were
so cold to me.'

'I didn't say I was pleased about it,' Sven said,
amused. 'You were not in my game plan at all, let me
tell you.'

'Oh, your rules,' she said, standing on tiptoe to kiss

his chin. 'How you scared me with your rules. I thought I'd never measure up. I just wasn't sophisticated enough.'

'Is that why you wouldn't come and see me?' he asked soberly.

Gaby stared. 'Wouldn't come and see you?' she echoed.

His smile was crooked. 'I knew I had to leave you alone for a while. I'd frightened you and I'd accused you unjustly. I owed you some space. But I thought when I sent you the dress you'd at least get in touch.'

Gaby frowned. 'What dress?'

'Not that one.' His eyes swept up and down it in a look of admiration which made her blush again. 'You look highly sophisticated in that piece of nonsense. And deeply desirable. No, it was an evening dress intended to cover you from head to toe so you didn't go round seducing men by looking like a gypsy again.'

The spring-green dress! No wonder her employers had looked embarrassed when she'd thanked them for it. She told him. Sven began to laugh.

'All right,' he said eventually. 'I accept that was a genuine mistake. But why wouldn't you come and see me when your father asked you to?'

Gaby blinked. 'I thought he was advising me to make a fool of myself all over again,' she said. 'He's always urging me to be adventurous. Are you saying that was a message from you?'

'A coded message.'

She shook her head. 'Well, I didn't crack the code.'

He looked remorseful. 'And I thought you were telling me I'd hurt you too badly. That you really did never want to see me again. I—had to accept that.'

Gaby looked down at the possessive hand at her waist.

'You accepting it?' she enquired politely.

He gave a soft laugh. 'Ah, but I saw your photograph in the paper. It was a review of your South Bank recital.

Do you remember, that last evening, you told me that
you'd meant everything you'd said and done with me?
And that I might remember that when I saw your
photograph in the paper one day?' His voice was husky.
'Well, I did. And I remembered how you had been in
my arms——'

The kiss was almost fierce. Gaby felt as if her ribs
were cracking but she never wanted it to end. When
Sven's grip finally eased, she gave a long sigh of pure
happiness.

'This was how it was,' she murmured contentedly.
'Before you got your beastly attack of conscience, I
mean.'

His eyes gleamed. 'It was indeed. And you aren't
sending me away this time.'

Her arms tightened round him. 'I didn't send you
away last time. But you looked so horrified. . .' She
flinched from the memory. 'I thought you'd betrayed
someone by taking me to bed.'

'I thought I had,' Sven said soberly. 'You.' He
feathered a kiss over her hair. 'When I think of what
had happened to you and then I——'

Gaby silenced him by putting her fingers gently
against his lips.

'Sven, listen,' she said. 'It happened to me three
years ago, the thing with Tim. It had been festering. I
should have talked about it before—but somehow I
never found that I could. So you were the first person I
told.'

Sven went very still, his hand cradling her shoulder.

'The only person, actually,' Gaby went on steadily.
'Ever. So, you see, you were already healing me.' She
turned her head and touched her mouth to the back of
his hand. 'You didn't hurt me or frighten me. You
made me feel alive again. Oh, I wish I could make you
understand.'

'I do,' he said quietly.

She looked up and met his eyes. She saw that he did.

He smiled faintly, tracing an eyebrow with a gentle finger.

'You did the same for me, my Gaby. You lectured me and shouted at me and made me feel again. I'd been in deep-freeze for years, without realising it.'

Gaby looked at him wonderingly. He mimed a kiss.

'But you knew that, didn't you?' His arms tightened. 'Marry me,' he said roughly. 'I need you. God knows I do. Without you, it's worth nothing.'

'Oh, darling,' said Gaby. She reached up and brought his head down. 'I think you'd better take me home now,' she said against his mouth. 'Your home,' she explained to make her meaning crystal-clear. Before her breath was wholly cut off she added, 'And make an honest woman of me before I become an old maid.'

'It will be a pleasure,' Sven assured her.

Welcome to Europe

SWEDEN — 'land of lakes and forests'

For those of you who enjoy the great outdoors there can be no better holiday destination than Sweden — a country just waiting to be explored. Whatever your mood, Sweden can cater for it — you can visit the bustling and elegant cities, go climbing in the mountains, walk or cycle through the fields and forests, canoe along one of the numerous waterways, or simply swim and sunbathe at a lakeside. It's the ideal place in which to unwind and take life at your own pace, while enjoying the welcoming warmth and friendliness of the people.

THE ROMANTIC PAST

Distant ancestors of the Swedish people were fishermen and seamen who used the sea, lakes and rivers to travel through their densely forested lands. Later, the people who became known as **Vikings** embarked on long sea voyages that took them all over the then known world.

Towards the end of the 19th century and in the early years of the 20th century over one million Swedes —

about a quarter of the population — left the poor agricultural areas — especially Värmland, Småland and Bohuslän — for the Swedish-speaking communities of Wisconsin and Minnesota, USA. This mass exodus coincided with the beginning of Sweden's Industrial Revolution, and the government were forced to acknowledge that the country was losing large numbers of young, able-bodied citizens. Consequently, a survey was set up in 1908, which revealed that the Swedish people were strongly dissatisfied with life in their country, and henceforth led to changes and reforms designated to encourage Swedes either to stay in or return to their homeland.

Until the Second World War Sweden was largely a homogenous nation — although many Swedes emigrated, immigrants were rare. However, Sweden's years of prosperity after World War II attracted a deluge of newcomers from Finland, southern Europe — political refugees mainly — and indeed from all over the world, so that one in eight Swedes born today is of immigrant descent.

In Sweden every province, as well as many districts and villages, has its own version of the national folk costume, although basically it comprises knee breeches, embroidered waistcoat and felt hat for the men, and flared skirt, apron, waistcoat and bonnet for the women. Floral patterns embroidered on a girl's waistcoat indicate her place of birth and marital status! This costume is so widely recognised in Sweden that people still choose to wear it on formal occasions, keeping the tradition alive.

One of the most popular festive occasions in Sweden is **Midsummer Eve**, and there are several folk traditions associated with this holiday. Homes, churches, auditoria, even cars are decorated with garlands of flowers and leaves, and almost every town and village has a maypole, raised mid-afternoon, around which people dance. Midsummer Eve is also regarded as a night of magical powers and supernatural happenings. It is believed that it is possible to find out whom you will marry by picking a bunch of seven or nine different varieties of flowers from as many meadows or ditches then placing it under your pillow. That night you will dream of your bride- or groom-to-be. The dew collected on this night is also said to contain special properties which can cure illnesses.

Famous people from Sweden include the pop group **Abba**, **Ingmar Bergman**, **Bjorn Borg**, **Stefan Edberg**, children's author **Astrid Lindgren**, and artists **Carl Larsson** and **Anders Zorn**.

THE ROMANTIC PRESENT — pastimes for lovers. . .

Since one of Sweden's most prominent attractions is its glorious countryside and scenery, what better place to focus on than the region of **Dalarna**, the heart of the so-called **Folklore District**? Here, Sweden's ancient rural traditions are maintained more strongly than in almost any other part of the country.

A good place to begin your exploration of Dalarna is at the provincial capital of **Falun**, where copper mining has thrived for some 900 years. This is where the red ochre which forms the basis for the distinctive paint used on buildings all over the country is produced, and you can't miss the so-called 'Great Pit', an enormous hole in the ground which has been there since 1687, when the entire copper mine caved in. If you don't mind getting a bit grubby, and you're not claustrophobic, you can don overalls and a helmet and take a guided tour down into sections of the old mine workings—an interesting but grim reminder of the conditions under which miners once worked.

A short trip from Falun will take you to the nearby picturesque village of **Sundborn**, where you might like to take a tour around the lovely lakeside home of the well-known Swedish artist **Carl Larsson**, who lived here at the beginning of the century. His simple paintings depicting his happy family life were influenced greatly by the local folk-art traditions.

From Sundborn head for the huge **Lake Siljan**—the largest and most beautiful lake in Dalarna. At the lakeside town of **Rättvik** you will find a magnificent church, huge in relation to the other buildings in the town. Parts of the church date back to the 13th century and inside there are several folk-art paintings on display.

A romantic tour of the towns and villages flanking **Lake Siljan** is a must for visitors—there is so much to see and the lake is surrounded by breathtaking scenery. On leaving Rättvik it is well worth making a brief stop at a hill called **Röjeråsen**—the lookout tower here affords a truly magnificent view of the lake that is bound to inspire you to explore the area further!

Still only a short distance from Rättvik you'll find the village of **Nusnäs**, an essential stop-off point for buying souvenirs, since this is where the traditional, brightly painted Dalarna **wood-carved horses** are made. But don't spend too much money here—save some for the many other souvenirs on offer around Sweden, including Swedish **glass**, which is famous throughout the world, **ceramics**, **textiles**, **leather goods** and inexpensive, high-quality **kitchenware**. Wherever you go, you're sure to find something you'll want to take home with you.

Next, why don't you make your way to the **Grönklitt
bear sanctuary** near **Orsa**? Here you can see the animals
in a natural forest habitat — from a safe distance of
course!

Mora is the next port of call to head for. This small,
elegant town has a museum housing the work of the
Swedish artist **Anders Zorn**, as well as his home and
studio, which are open to the public. From here you
might like to visit the island of **Sollerön**, on the western
side of the lake, where the **Siljan church boats** —
resembling the ancient Viking longships — are built and
there is an impressive 18th-century church, as well as a
handicrafts centre.

Continuing your journey to the southern end of Lake
Siljan, you will come to the popular holiday resort of
Leksand. This small town comes to life in the summer,
and the church here is famous for its Midsummer
celebrations. Indeed, Dalarna as a whole attracts thousands of visitors each year at Midsummer, and wherever
you are you can expect to see many of the locals in
their colourful traditional costumes. In addition, if your
visit to Leksand happens to coincide with the first
Sunday in July then you will see the **festival of the
church boats**. Originally used to transport Sunday wor-
shippers from the surrounding area, these boats make
an impressive spectacle. Another cultural attraction at
this time of year is the open-air performance of a
traditional mystery play known as *Himlaspelet*, staged
by the local people.

And finally, to complete your tour of Lake Siljan, why
not make for **Tällberg** — a small, typical Dalarna village
with traditional timber buildings and even a maypole?
Here you can enjoy a leisurely stroll with your lover at
the end of the day, down to the lakeside, where you

can soak up the atmosphere as the sun goes down over the shimmering, gently lapping water. . .

After all this fresh air and exercise you'll be bound to have a healthy appetite which Swedish fare is bound to satisfy! Sweden is renowned for its traditional *smörgåsbord*—a kind of buffet meal comprising a variety of tasty dishes. **Herrings** are especially popular, as are open sandwiches, beautifully prepared with all kinds of fish, meat and sausages. But those of you who enjoy fish will be delighted to know that the Swedes are great fish eaters, and you can expect to find **salmon**, **trout**, **grayling** and **perch** on the menu, as well as a wide selection of **shellfish**. Swedish meatballs known as *köttbullar* are also very tasty, and you might like to try **'Jansson's Temptation'**—a gratin of potatoes, cream, onions and anchovies. Restaurants in the north especially also offer a number of **reindeer dishes** so, for those of you who have never tried it, now's your chance!

In the rural regions you might also find examples of Swedish home cooking such as **pea soup with pancakes** or *Pytt i Panna*—'Put in the Pan'—basically a huge fry-up.

For dessert you can choose from sweet **pancakes**, **cake** or **gateau**, or **fresh fruit**.

Alcohol is extremely expensive in Sweden, and usually the Swedes drink either milk or beer with their meals. However, spirits are very popular, and schnapps— **snaps**—is considered an essential aperitif for a really good meal.

DID YOU KNOW THAT. . .?

*   with an area of 174,000 square miles (450,000 km) Sweden is the fourth largest country in Europe, stretch-

ing for almost 1,000 miles (1,600 km) from south to north.

* Sweden has 96,000 **lakes**.

* there is no law of trespass in Sweden, access to the countryside being governed by a centuries-old tradition known as *Allemansrätt* ('Everyman's Right'). This basically means that anyone can, within reason, walk, ride, ski or camp anywhere in the countryside.

* Sweden's **exports** include wood, cellulose, paper, iron ore, machines and instruments and chemical products.

* the currency of Sweden is the **krona**.

* to say 'I love you' in Swedish say '*Jag älskar dig*'.

SUMMER SPECIAL!

Four exciting new Romances for the price of three

Each Romance features British heroines and their encounters with dark and desirable Mediterranean men. *Plus, a free Elmlea recipe booklet inside every pack.*

So sit back and enjoy your sumptuous summer reading pack and indulge yourself with the free Elmlea recipe ideas.

Available July 1994   Price £5.70

THREE TIMES A LOVE STORY

A special collection of three individual love stories from one of the world's best-loved romance authors. This beautiful volume offers a unique chance for new fans to sample some of Janet Dailey's earlier works and for long-time fans to collect an edition to treasure.

WORLDWIDE

AVAILABLE NOW

PRICED £4.99

Accept 4 FREE Romances and 2 FREE gifts

FROM READER SERVICE

Here's an irresistible invitation from Mills & Boon. Please accept our offer of 4 FREE Romances, a CUDDLY TEDDY and a special MYSTERY GIFT! Then, if you choose, go on to enjoy 6 captivating Romances every month for just £1.90 each, postage and packing FREE. Plus our FREE Newsletter with author news, competitions and much more.

Send the coupon below to:
Mills & Boon Reader Service,
FREEPOST, PO Box 236,
Croydon, Surrey CR9 9EL.

- - - - - - ▶ NO STAMP REQUIRED ◀ - - - - - - - - - - - - - - - - - - -

Yes!

Please rush me 4 FREE Romances and 2 FREE gifts! Please also reserve me a Reader Service subscription. If I decide to subscribe I can look forward to receiving 6 brand new Romances for just £11.40 each month, post and packing FREE. If I decide not to subscribe I shall write to you within 10 days - I can keep the free books and gifts whatever I choose. I may cancel or suspend my subscription at any time. I am over 18 years of age.

Ms/Mrs/Miss/Mr _____   EP70R

Address _____

_____

Postcode _____   Signature _____